A Cadenza
for
Caruso

Also available in Large Print
by Barbara Paul:

The Renewable Virgin

A Cadenza for Caruso

BARBARA PAUL

G.K.HALL &CO.
Boston, Massachusetts
1986

LP

Published in Large Print by arrangement with
St. Martin's Press.

G. K. Hall Large Print Book Series.

Set in 16 pt Plantin.

Library of Congress Cataloging in Publication Data

Paul, Barbara, 1931-
  A cadenza for Caruso.

  (G.K. Hall large print book series)
  Caruso, Enrico, 1873–1921– Fiction. 2. Puccini,
Giacomo, 1858–1924– Fiction. 3. Large type books.
1. Title.
[PS3566.A82615C3 1986]   813'.54   85-27216
ISBN 0-8161-3781-1 (lg. print)

For my family —
The Trabers in California
and the Pauls in Massachusetts

ONE

THE ACOUSTICS WERE not good. The sight-lines were terrible. The stage was cavernous and hard to light, the dressing rooms were windowless and none too clean, the backstage area was cramped and inadequate.

Enrico Caruso sighed in contentment. Beautiful, simply beautiful.

He swaggered out to center stage and struck a heroic pose for the empty auditorium. Before long that famous Diamond Horseshoe would be ablaze with light, packed with New Yorkers eager to hear him sing again. Caruso always felt at home in the Metropolitan Opera House. Covent Garden was more glamorous, La Scala had the blessings of tradition behind it — but the Metropolitan was his kingdom.

A man can be forgiven for strutting a little in his own kingdom.

A discreet cough from the wings ended the moment. "What is it, Ugo?" Caruso called out.

"There is no running water backstage," his valet answered. "How can I make the dressing room clean when there is no running water backstage?"

"Of course there is running water backstage. There has been running water here for years and years." Two years.

"It is not running *now*, Rico," Ugo said glumly. "Everywhere is dirt and dust and no water."

The tenor waved his arms in the air. "Then find the running-water expert! Take care of this terrible problem!" The valet muttered something under his breath and disappeared. *Martino would know what to do*, Caruso thought in exasperation. But Martino was back at the hotel.

"Ah, Enrico! You are here, you are here!" A familiar voice floated out of the dark auditorium as its owner came down the aisle toward the stage. Giulio Gatti-Casazza, general manager of the Metropolitan Opera, had met Caruso's ship a few days earlier;

but now, on the stage of the Met, they greeted each other as if after a ten-year separation.

"Mr. Gatti!" Caruso said affectionately. He liked working with Gatti-Casazza. The previous manager had had no real understanding of opera or, even worse, of opera singers. But Mr. Gatti knew what terrible hardships singers had to face. Mr. Gatti knew everything.

"The new opera— it progresses, yes?" Gatti-Casazza wanted to know.

"It is all in here," Caruso said solemnly, tapping his forehead. "It is here," grasping his throat dramatically, "that the trouble lies."

Gatti-Casazza's eyes grew wide. "The voice . . . ?"

"An annoyingly persistent sore throat," the tenor said worriedly. "Everything irritates it— smoke, dust . . ." Then he remembered. "Ugo says there is no running water backstage. Dust everywhere— "

"Ah yes, a small problem with the plumbing," the general manager said soothingly. "Soon to be remedied, I am assured. If your man can wait a little while . . . ? Good. But tell me, Enrico, what are you doing for your throat?"

"My special spray, gargles, I wear amber beads around my neck—"

"You are smoking those strong Egyptian cigarettes still?"

Caruso grinned sheepishly. "I use a holder."

Gatti-Casazza waved a finger at him admonishingly. "That is the cause of your sore throat, Enrico! Put the cigarettes aside, at least until after the première. You owe that much to Puccini." His face darkened. "We must do all we can to ease his burden."

Caruso nodded in sober agreement. The composer was coming to New York to supervise the world première of his new opera— an occasion for joy and celebration under normal circumstances. But Puccini would be arriving under a cloud, still suffering the effects of a shocking scandal that at one point had driven him close to suicide. Puccini had said that working on the new opera was all that kept him sane.

"I will undertake to cheer him up," Caruso announced expansively. "I am very good at cheering people up."

"That you are, Enrico," the other man laughed, "that you are. Puccini's ship arrives

4

early tomorrow morning, by the way. You will have a few days before we begin work in earnest."

"I work every day," Caruso proclaimed. "Even on Sundays."

The general manager was plucking at his beard — a familiar signal that something was bothering him. "Enrico — no tricks this time. No little surprises for the other singers. I want your word. No practical jokes at all."

Caruso was hurt. "You think I play jokes when we prepare a new opera?"

"No filling the other singers' hats with flour. No nailing of oranges to the table."

"There are no oranges in the new opera."

"Whatever. I want you to promise me you will play no pranks at all."

"Such a promise is not necessary," the tenor said with offended dignity, "but I give it just the same."

Gatti-Casazza's smile of relief was so dazzling that Caruso forgave him on the spot. "I believe you, Enrico. We will have good rehearsals — and a great performance, yes?"

The tenor decided to leave poor Ugo to cope with the dirty dressing room as best he could; he himself would walk back to the

Hotel Knickerbocker — only two short blocks away, overlooking Times Square, the "crossroads of the world." Caruso liked being in the center of things. No lover of exercise, Caruso nevertheless enjoyed strolling the streets of New York. It was a crisp, bright day in November, the year was 1910, and all was right with the world.

He hadn't gone a full block before some stranger was pounding him on the back and calling him *primo tenore*. He was, of course, *primo* — but it was always gratifying to hear someone say so. Caruso talked to the man in Italian, delighted as always with the polyglot nature of New York's citizenry. He himself slipped in an English sentence now and then; he always did, when talking in Italian — good practice. The back-thumping stranger had been born in Milan and had on more than one occasion heard Caruso sing at La Scala. He didn't ask for money, so Caruso didn't offer any; they parted on friendly terms.

But in the lobby of the Hotel Knickerbocker a supplicant did lie in wait. Another stranger and another Italian, but this one was shabby and defeated-looking. Caruso listened sympathetically to the man's hard-luck story, and then with a grandiose gesture handed him a moderate sum of money. He basked momentarily in the outpouring of gratitude that followed; when the supplicant had left, Caruso pulled out a small notebook and carefully wrote down the amount he had given away. Keeping accounts was important.

Caruso pushed open the door to his hotel apartment. "Martino! Mario! Barthélemy!" The three other members of his entourage (beside Ugo) came running. "Mario, my throat spray. Martino, a hot bath and clean clothes. Use the jasmine scent." To Barthélemy: "After the bath, we work."

Barthélemy smiled. "We work on the end of the first act?"

"Yes, yes, we work on the end of the first act," Caruso flapped a hand at him. "And Martino— arrange with the management for a small dinner party tomorrow night. The great Puccini should not spend his first evening in New York alone. Let's see— we ask Amato, Scotti, Crispano . . ." He counted on his fingers. "Eight people."

"I will take care of it, Rico," Martino said. Caruso put the matter out of his mind; once Martino knew about it, the dinner party was as good as arranged. Martino had been with him longer than anybody else and was in charge of the other valets. In fact, he was in charge of almost everything.

Young Mario came hurrying in with the throat spray. *Ah, that felt good.* Caruso tried a high note, sprayed some more. "Let us have slightly more glycerine in the next batch, Mario."

The young man's mournful eyes peered out beneath his mop of thick dark hair. "I will mix it up this very day, signore." Polite boy, Mario— he couldn't quite bring himself to say *Rico* as the others did. A little too solemn for one so young, but *very* polite.

Caruso luxuriated in his scented bath for almost an hour, eating ice cream and smoking the strong cigarettes Gatti-Casazza had warned him about. He dressed in his second outfit of the day and would probably change one more time: a singer had to be careful of infection.

Time to work. First the breathing exercises. Then the scales, for warm-up. Then the music.

Five years earlier Giacomo Puccini had seen a play in New York called *The Girl of the Golden West* and had been impressed by it. So impressed, in fact, that he'd made it the basis of his new opera — *La Fanciulla del West*. To Caruso this was one of the most exotic operas he'd ever appeared in. A rowdy saloon scene, a card game with life-or-death stakes, a manhunt, a lynching party, live horses on stage, California gold miners, cowboys and Indians, outlaws, vigilantes — everything about the Gold Rush and America's Old West that was *so* exciting! Caruso was singing the role of the dashing bandit Ramerrez, and Gatti-Casazza had promised him he would indeed be packing a six-shooter.

Barthélemy was seated at the gold-and-white Empire-style piano. "The end of the first act," he announced firmly.

Caruso shrugged acquiescence. Barthélemy was more than just an accompanist; he was an excellent musician in his own right. And if Barthélemy felt that the end of the first act needed work, then the end of the first act needed work. Caruso knew when to listen.

He sang, half-voice, repeating phrases over and over until he and Barthélemy both were satisfied. The music was something of a departure for Puccini. Gatti-Casazza was excited about the score; he'd said it was more mature and more dramatic than Puccini's earlier work. *It's certainly harder to sing*, Caruso thought. More augmented intervals, more dissonance. The tenor liked it.

This was the music Puccini had labored over to keep himself from committing suicide. An opera that grew out of such pain could not be the same sweetly romantic kind of melody the Italian lyric theatre had loved for so many years. Melody there was aplenty in *La Fanciulla del West,* but there was also dissonance.

Elvira.

Dissonance, Elvira — how quickly one word called up the other! It was Elvira Puccini who'd caused all the trouble.

"Rico," Barthélemy said reprovingly, "you're not concentrating."

Caruso announced a small intermission and called to Mario for his throat spray.

It was Elvira's jealousy of her famous and handsome husband that had brought about the tragedy. Of course, one could say Puccini had given her plenty of cause — but not this time, not really. Puccini had been carrying on a mild flirtation with a young servant girl named Doria, right there in his own home in the village Torre del Lago. Elvira had accused the two of having an affair and drove the girl out of the house.

For weeks Elvira spread rumors about the girl, taunting her publicly in the streets of Torre del Lago, calling her names a respectable married woman wasn't supposed to know. Aware of Puccini's reputation with the ladies, many of the villagers believed Elvira's accusations. Even Doria's family began to doubt her.

At last young Doria — hardly more than a child — could bear no more . . . and took a lethal dose of poison. Elvira had literally hounded the girl to death. A life had ended, all because of a flirtation that meant nothing to Puccini.

"Shall we resume?" Barthélemy asked.

But it hadn't ended there. Doria's family had ordered an autopsy, and the examination proved the girl had died a virgin — whereupon the family brought charges of persecution and defamation of character against Elvira Puccini. Elvira was tried and convicted; but before the sentence was carried out, the composer had been able to buy Doria's family off, bribing them into withdrawing the charges. Only in that way had he been able to prevent his wife's going to prison.

Despair over this tragic sequence of events had driven Puccini to the brink of taking his own life. His music had saved him; he'd buried himself in work, orchestrating his private anguish into the new opera— including that achingly beautiful aria in the last act.

Caruso turned to Barthélemy. *"Ch'ella mi creda,"* he ordered.

Barthélemy gave him a lopsided smile. "Rico, you already sing that one perfectly. In your sleep, you can sing it perfectly."

"So, I will sing it perfectly *now*. Play!"

The accompanist sighed in resignation, found the place in the score, and began to play.

Ch'ella mi creda libero e lontano. Let her believe I am free and far away. Caruso sang full voice, holding back nothing—treating his neighbors in the Hotel Knickerbocker to a free concert. A short aria, but a touching one.

Applause greeted the conclusion: Martino was standing in the doorway, his face one big smile. "Bravo, Rico, bravo!"

The tenor bowed.

"A letter has arrived for you by messenger," Martino said. "A letter with the most delicious scent of violets arising from it!"

"An answer to my invitation!" Caruso beamed. "Where is it?"

Martino handed him an envelope, addressed in a delicate spidery handwriting in lavender ink.

Dear Mr. Caruso,

I want to thank you for the lovely American beauty roses you sent; they are my favorites. How did you know? Frankly, I am surprised you remembered me from last year; we barely had a chance to speak on that occasion. And yes, I would be most pleased to have dinner with you. If you care to call for me at seven this evening, I shall be waiting.

Caroline N.

"Ah, Ca-ro-*lee*-na, *bellissima!*" Caruso kissed the note and waved it in the air. "Martino! My dinner clothes — the blue!"

Just then Ugo walked in, covered with dust from head to foot. "Your dressing room is clean, Rico," he grumbled. "Why do I always get the dirty jobs?" Martino hustled him out while Mario quickly sprayed the room with perfume.

But Ugo's unsanitary presence couldn't dim Caruso's anticipation of the evening. Nowhere was he so happy as in New York. He was surrounded by friends. Strangers came up to him on the street, full of praise and extravagant compliments. Charming young ladies wrote him notes saying *yes*. His career was at its peak, and his voice had darkened to the point where he could now sing heroic roles as well as lyric ones. The great Puccini had survived his ordeal and the result was a new opera in which he, Enrico Caruso himself, would create the lead tenor role, in the opera house he preferred to all others in the world.

No clouds on the horizon anywhere. Caruso was rich, famous, and loved. Not bad for a poor boy from the slums of Naples.

The next day Caruso dressed carefully for his visit to Puccini. After consulting with Martino, he'd attired his portly self in a fawn-colored suit, bright green checked waistcoat, curly-brimmed hat, gold-headed cane, and yellow gloves. There. That should do it.

He was a little nervous. The tenor hadn't seen Puccini for a while, not since the scandal of Doria's death had made every newspaper in Italy. But Caruso hadn't been completely comfortable with the composer even before that.

Puccini was a hard man to please. He'd withheld permission for Caruso to sing his *Bohème* for an insultingly long time. And he never hesitated to criticize a singer's performance — any singer, and performance. But when he was pleased — ah, when he was pleased, then he was most generous with his praise. He'd said some wonderfully ego-building things to Caruso on occasion. The trouble was, one never knew what to expect from him. The tenor would have liked to have the composer as a friend, but there had always been a distance between them.

The last Caruso had heard, Puccini was more or less reconciled with his wife; but the tenor didn't know whether Elvira had come with her husband to New York or not. A touchy situation. What was the proper behavior in such circumstances? Should he offer his condolences for the young servant girl's death, or his congratulations that Elvira did not have to go to prison? It didn't occur to Caruso not to bring the subject up at all.

"I am ready," he announced to Martino.

The head valet looked him over carefully. "Yes, you are ready."

Puccini's hotel, the Buckingham, was ten blocks away, too much for Caruso. Ugo was waiting on the street with one of the new taximetre motor cabs; Caruso rather enjoyed riding the horse trolleys and the electric streetcars, but automobiles were even more fun. He examined the one in front of him critically. "Ugo, do you think you could learn to drive a motor car?"

"I? Never!" the valet shuddered. "Those things are not safe." Caruso shrugged and climbed into the cab. Ugo slammed the door after him. "When will you be back, Rico?"

"After lunch sometime. Tell Barthélemy we work then." That was habit speaking; Barthélemy already knew.

Caruso's nervousness increased as the cab chugged up Seventh Avenue, and the driver's constant chatter didn't help. He paid the driver double the fare the man asked (carefully recording the amount in his notebook), and with something less than his usual swagger walked into the Hotel Buckingham. Outside Puccini's door, he took a deep breath, tried to count to ten but gave up at four, and knocked.

A stranger opened the door. "Well, Caruso, you are looking prosperous. Come in, come in." Only when he heard the voice did Caruso realize the stranger was Puccini.

The tenor was shocked at the change in the other man. Puccini had lost a lot of weight. His tanned cheeks were hollowed and showed deep furrows. His once vigorous handshake was now flabby and uncertain.

"Puccini!" Caruso shouted. "You are ill!"

"Not any more," the composer smiled sadly. "Come sit down, Caruso. Tell me what you have been doing."

"You have a doctor in New York?" the tenor asked worriedly. "I can recommend one, a very strict man but a good physician."

Puccini shook his head. "It's not that kind of illness. It is a sickness of the spirit. But that too passes." He pulled out chairs for Caruso and himself. Much of the floor space was taken up by two unopened steamer trunks. "I am sorry I cannot offer you anything. I sent my valet out for wine over an hour ago and he is not yet returned. He is new, you see— he has never been in America before."

"Eh, well, he is probably lost. New York can be confusing to a newcomer." Caruso paused. "You do not look well, my friend."

"He'll find his way back," Puccini said, ignoring Caruso's last remark. "Now tell me, what else besides *Fanciulla* do you sing at the Metropolitan this season?"

But Caruso wouldn't let him change the subject. "Are you certain you do not need a doctor? They have medicine for everything these days."

"Do they have a pill that can change the past?" Puccini snapped angrily. Then: "Forgive me, Caruso, I am not as even-tempered as I used to be."

Caruso had never found him particularly even-tempered to begin with but politely refrained from saying so. He glanced into another room of the suite. "Is Elvira here?"

"No."

Caruso's face fell. "I am sorry to hear that. I had thought you . . . she . . ." He floundered, not knowing how to finish.

"I did not want her to come," Puccini said, "and she resents me for that, too. I just need some time away from her, you understand? Doria's death is still very much between us. And I am to blame! I!"

"You?" Caruso was surprised. "But it was Elvira who caused all the, the trouble!"

"Not entirely. I did not seduce the girl, as Elvira thought—but I am not guiltless in the matter."

"But all married men have these little flirts," Caruso protested. "Italian wives understand these things! It is nothing to break up a marriage over."

Puccini shook his head. "Elvira is a very unhappy woman. She feels left out. True, I've not always been as discreet as I should have been—but I have always gone back to her! She knows I always come back!"

"Always, yes."

"It is the relatives," Puccini said bitterly. "Always the house is full of her relatives— to keep her company, she says, when I am away. *They* put her up to it. They like to make trouble. They see me exchanging a few pleasantries with young Doria and they tell Elvira we are sleeping together."

"So it is really the relatives' fault!"

"No, I am the one responsible. Doria would be alive today if I had kept a proper distance and given no cause for suspicion. *I* killed her."

"No no no no *no!*" Caruso cried. "You must not blame yourself! You did not make Elvira persecute the girl—she did that herself. With a little help from the relatives."

"And from me," Puccini added glumly. "We are all to blame for that girl's death. Doria was the only truly innocent one in the whole . . . ," his voice trailed off. "Caruso! Do you know what you have done? You have made me talk about it!"

"That is good?"

"I do not know, I think perhaps it is. All I want to do is hide, bury myself in work. When the newspapers made headline stories out of what happened—eh, you know how I hate strangers intruding into my life. It has been like living in hell, with all the devils pointing their fingers at me! But now here I am talking to you about it, and it seems the most natural thing in the world!"

"Then that *is* good," Caruso pronounced judicially. "What's done is done, and we must learn to live with it." He was feeling grandfatherly and wise. "Look to the future. Look to December tenth! The tenth of December, nineteen ten — a date to remember!"

Puccini smiled tentatively. "Let us hope so, Caruso." The tenth was the date of the première of *La Fanciulla del West*.

They talked of the new opera for a while, and Caruso was cheered to see Puccini begin to show a spark of his old enthusiasm. Then the tenor told the other man he was throwing a little dinner party for him that night at the Hotel Knickerbocker. Puccini tried to beg off, but Caruso wouldn't hear of it. "Only your friends will be there," he told the composer, "old friends who wish you well."

Puccini finally agreed.

"Now then," Caruso said, pushing his luck, "why not come have lunch with me? I wish to introduce you to the Café Martin. They make such a nice oily spaghetti — the kind you rarely find away from home." His mouth began to water.

"It sounds wonderful — but, alas, I have an appointment. Toscanini will be here shortly. We need to consult about the score." The two men exchanged a wry look; they'd both locked horns with the Maestro before. But it was unthinkable that any other conductor should be entrusted with the new opera.

"Until tonight then," Caruso said, not particularly eager to run into Toscanini just yet. He left the composer feeling slightly better than he had, and he knew it. Caruso was good at cheering people up.

Down on the street Caruso hesitated. Perhaps Puccini's turning down his luncheon invitation was a good thing. The oily spaghetti the Café Martin served was one of the things his doctor had warned him against—that same strict doctor Caruso had earlier tried to recommend to Puccini. *Eat less and exercise,* the doctor had said, and he'd said it in a way that made the tenor listen. Bravely Caruso started the ten-block walk back to the Hotel Knickerbocker.

What a strange man Puccini was! Blaming himself for what Elvira had done. Well, he knew more of what went on in his own household than Caruso did; maybe he was a little bit to blame at that. Puccini had actually thought of killing himself during that dark time, something Caruso hadn't quite had the nerve to ask the other man about. But he didn't seem suicidal now. *Everything will be all right,* the tenor told himself. And believed it.

Soon he was puffing and starting to sweat. He looked up at the street sign: he'd come two blocks. Two long blocks, though, not those nice easy north-south short ones. Caruso had always thought of himself as a solidly built man, but that doctor had kept using the word *fat* every time he saw him. Not *overweight,* but *fat.* Caruso's English wasn't all that good, but he understood the distinction.

He started walking again. The dinner party that evening was all arranged; he'd checked with Martino that morning. American steaks with lobster, and several kinds of pasta to make Puccini feel at home.

Pasta.

Caruso stepped to the curb and signaled a cab. "Broadway and Twenty-fifth," he told the driver. "The Café Martin." Some things you just can't fight.

"Caruso!" the driver cried when he recognized his famous passenger. *"Caro* Caruso!" Another Italian, which meant another fan. Driver and passenger chugged down Broadway, Caruso happily humming *Celeste Aïda* as he rode.

The dinner party did its job; Puccini's mood was lightening with each new course. In the corner of the Knickerbocker dining room, the big table set with white linen and gleaming silverware was ringing with laughter and rapidly spoken Italian. The composer's color seemed better, and his eyes had some life in them again. Caruso congratulated himself (and Martino) on a job well done.

On the other side of Puccini sat baritone Pasquale Amato, one of Caruso's closest friends and a steadying man to have around. Amato was singing the role of the sheriff in *La Fanciulla del West,* the villainous lawman in pursuit of the hero bandit Caruso was playing. Amato looked the part; big and mustachioed, he almost always dressed in black. "Why do you not write an opera that lets the baritone get the girl?" Amato was asking the composer.

Puccini placed a hand over his heart and assumed a mock-noble expression. "I have too much respect for tradition. The tenor *always* gets the girl."

"Besides, baritones make such good villains," someone else at the table said.

"And fathers," Amato sighed. "Villains, fathers, and friend of the hero— my wife tells me that is my lot in life. Ah, well."

"Your wife is here with you?" Puccini asked.

"No, Rosa does not like to travel when she is expecting. She and the boys spend Christmas with her family."

"Your conference with Toscanini," Caruso asked the composer, "it goes well?"

"Remarkably well," Puccini answered, his surprise showing. "For the first time ever, we are in complete accord as to how the music is to be interpreted. Every time before, he fights me over every measure, every *note*— but not this time. This time he is so kind and gentle I cannot believe what I am hearing!"

"Hm," said Amato. "This is *Arturo* Toscanini we are speaking of, is it not?"

"Is there another?" Puccini laughed. "Yes, it is the same Toscanini who rages and screams and withers strong men with his sarcasm. Perhaps he is just showing me special consideration because of my trouble and it may not last— "

"It won't last," Caruso and Amato said together.

"Pity," said Puccini. "Such a pleasant change."

The first full rehearsal for *La Fanciulla del West* was to take place in just a few days; and between that time and the opening on December 10, Caruso was scheduled to sing in several other operas at the Metropolitan. Normally he would have refused to rehearse one opera during the day and sing another at night; he needed the day to prepare for his performance. But *Fanciulla* was a world première, after all— the very first the Met had ever presented. So how could he refuse? Especially when the new opera had been written by the world's greatest living composer. It occurred to Caruso that the Germans would say Richard Strauss was the greatest— but then, what did the Germans know of opera?

So there was very little time for play left. "Tomorrow," the tenor told Puccini, "we ride the ferry boat to Brooklyn— a nice trip, I go many times. When we get back, we stop at Dorlon's for oysters. Then . . . ah, an antiques dealer on Fifth Avenue tells me he has a pair of Alessandro Vittorio candlesticks — we go look at them, yes? For dinner, perhaps the roof garden at Madison Square Garden? We can watch a show as we dine!"

The composer laughed. "Caruso, do you never slow down? When do you find time for work?"

"Six hours every day," Caruso announced firmly. "First the breathing exercises, then the scales, then the music. Six hours I practice, every day."

"So he does," Amato nodded.

"And I also study translations of libretti to improve my English!" the tenor finished triumphantly.

"That is about all they are good for," Amato mused. "Why does anyone bother translating opera into English? No one is ever going to sing it. English is for *sports,* for playing tennis and golf and racing the horses. But for opera? Never."

Without thinking about it, Caruso started singing one of the airs from *Tosca* in English, making up the words when he couldn't remember the translation. The sweetly romantic tune seemed wonderfully incongruous when sung with words such as

Strange harmony of deliciously blending contrasts. Soon the whole table was laughing, and then the entire dining room of the Knickerbocker— and none was laughing harder than Puccini.

The dinner party did its job.

TWO

LATE FOR THE first day of rehearsal.

"You should have had the clothes laid out, Ugo," Caruso scolded as they hurried down Broadway. "Martino told you which ones last night."

"No, he didn't, Rico. He forgot."

"Martino *never* forgets. You are the one who forgot."

"You always take Martino's side against me," Ugo grumbled.

Thank goodness the Metropolitan was so close. For the first few days they would be working in a rehearsal hall with a piano accompanist, moving to the main stage with full orchestra only when they had the basics of the opera under control. Caruso *hoped* it would be in a few days' time; with Maestro Toscanini at the helm, one never knew.

The door to the rehearsal hall was standing open. Caruso stuck his head in and took a quick look around: Neither Toscanini nor the Met's general manager had yet arrived. The tenor sighed in relief. He didn't want to offend Gatti-Casazza; and like all singers, he was more than a little intimidated by Toscanini. Caruso gave his hat and coat to Ugo and told him not to make any disturbance during the rehearsal.

"I *never* make a disturbance during rehearsal," Ugo replied indignantly.

The hall was crowded; the fifty-man chorus took up a lot of room. The other two of the opera's three principals were already there; Pasquale Amato stood talking to Emmy Destinn, the soprano who was singing the title role. Ah, it was like old times! So many times the three of them had sung together before—*Aïda, Gioconda, Ballo in Maschera, Tosca.* It was always comfortable, performing with voices and personalities that were so familiar, so dependable.

"Emmy! *Carissima!*" Caruso advanced toward her with outstretched arms.

Emmy endured a warm Italian embrace. "Well, Rico, I see you are still living the good life." She poked him playfully in the stomach.

"I live the life of a Spartan!" Caruso protested. "To prepare for *Fanciulla*. After all, it is the first time we create a new opera together! Are you not excited?"

"Of course I'm excited," she smiled. "But this is a strange one, is it not? Not like *Tosca* or *Butterfly* at all."

"Puccini is not content to repeat what he has done before," Amato nodded. "Sometimes I wish he were."

"Rico," Emmy said sternly, "no practical jokes. Not during rehearsal and not during the performance. This is a première, after all."

Caruso placed one hand over his heart and raised the other in the air. "You may rest assured, dear Emmy, there will be no practical jokes." He lowered his hands. "Besides, Mr. Gatti already made me promise."

Just then Emmy's maid appeared in the doorway and gestured to her. The soprano excused herself and walked away from the two men.

Caruso watched her go. Emmy Destinn had put on a few pounds herself. Emmy had never been sylphlike, but now she was just plain stout. She was not homely, but she was not exactly a beauty either. Could a woman with her stocky figure and middle-European mannerisms create the illusion of an American girl running a saloon in a mining camp? Of course she could, Caruso thought. She'd persuaded many a *Butterfly* audience that she was a delicate young geisha— so why not Minnie, girl of the Golden West? Frankly, Emmy looked like a cook. But when she sang— ah, when she sang, even the angels writhed in envy! "I adore that woman," Caruso sighed.

Amato smiled agreement.

Emmy came marching back, looking annoyed. "That woman. Such a fussbudget. A maid is supposed to *help*, not cause problems."

"I seem to recall your saying the same thing at Covent Garden," Amato remarked. "Why do you keep her if she is so much trouble?"

Emmy shrugged. "Habit. We are used to each other."

There was a stir in the room, and the three singers turned in time to see Toscanini make his entrance, followed by a beaming

Gatti-Casazza. Toscanini looked like a glittering-eyed, wild-crested bird of prey, ready to swoop down and peck the head of any singer who dared to be anything less than perfect.

After the preliminary exclamations and kissings were done with, Gatti-Casazza stood in the middle of the rehearsal hall — arms waving gently, asking for attention. It was his duty (and pleasure) to start things off with a little speech. He told the singers that *La Fanciulla del West* was the first world première ever to be staged at the Metropolitan Opera House and other things they already knew. He talked on for about ten minutes, saying nothing at all; but everyone enjoyed his little speech, because starting without one was unthinkable.

Then Toscanini took over. "I want you," he told the singers, "to think of this opera as an egg."

Caruso and Amato exchanged a glance.

"It is perfectly shaped," Toscanini explained, "and it has no seams. The arias are shorter and fewer and more integrated into the whole than in any other work Mr. Puccini has given us."

"Speaking of," Amato whispered,

"where is he?"

Caruso looked around. He hadn't noticed the composer was not there.

Toscanini started getting more specific, telling the principals, the supporting singers, and even the chorus exactly what was expected of them. That involved a departure from normal procedure. Choruses were usually rehearsed separately and not brought in until the last few rehearsals on stage. But the all-male *Fanciulla* chorus was a collective character in this opera, not just a human backdrop for the soloists to perform against. The chorus members were playing gold miners— riff-raff, crude and rough-spoken men as easily moved to sentimental tears as to violence.

The door opened and in walked Puccini — smiling, fashionably dressed, sure of his welcome. Everything came to a stop while there were more greetings, hand-shakings, back-clapping. Caruso's concentrated effort to cheer the composer up over the past few days had worked wonders. Puccini seemed at ease, handling several conversations at once. Caruso belatedly wondered what Toscanini thought of being upstaged in this way, but a glance in his direction showed the usually irascible conductor beaming benignly on the scene.

The hubbub eventually died down, but the unscheduled intermission had given Toscanini time to remember his egg metaphor. "I do not want an omelette!" he admonished them all firmly, to Puccini's bewilderment.

Eventually they got to the real business of the day: rehearsing the music. Toscanini followed his usual procedure of interrupting every few notes, waving his arms excitedly, singing along himself. But there were no bursts of temper, no sarcastic remarks.

"Do you suppose he is ill?" Caruso whispered.

"Give him time," Amato whispered back.

Caruso's character didn't enter until halfway through the first act. The tenor gestured to Ugo, who silently handed him the sketch pad he'd brought along. Caruso amused himself by making quick line drawings of the people around him. He sketched Toscanini, Puccini, Gatti-Casazza. He even did one of Ugo, sitting sleepily in the corner, bored by the constant repetition any early rehearsal involved. The drawing of Mr. Gatti turned out especially well.

With his droopy eyelids and square jaw and funny-looking beard, the Met's general manager was a natural for caricature. Caruso signed each drawing with a flourish; his signature was becoming almost as well known as the drawings themselves.

Emmy Destinn ducked a high C. The Maestro merely nodded, knowing she could hit it when the time came; even Toscanini didn't demand full-voice renditions at the first rehearsal. Emmy had learned the role in only twenty days, studying ten hours a day—six with Toscanini, four alone. She didn't even look tired.

Almost time for the bandit's entrance; Caruso put the sketch pad aside and signaled to Ugo for his throat spray. The pianist played the syncopated bandit theme and Caruso managed to sing about fourteen notes before Toscanini interrupted him.

Pasquale Amato missed a cue and came in a beat late. Toscanini screeched and made him do it over twice. Amato knew the music as well as Caruso did; he just hadn't seen the Maestro's long finger pointing at him.

Every singer in the room was willing to go along with Toscanini's eccentricities because they all knew they'd end up sounding better because of it. Conducting opera had generally been considered hack work until recently. Earlier Metropolitan managements had been content to hire any second-rate musician available to beat time for the orchestra, under the theory that opera-goers didn't buy tickets to look at the conductor's back. But when Gatti-Casazza had given up his position at La Scala to take over the Met, he'd brought Toscanini with him.

Under Toscanini, the whole nature of rehearsing opera was changed. The Maestro was determined to mold soloists, chorus, and orchestra into an artistic whole—and if that meant riding roughshod over some tender egos, then so be it! A musical Napoleon, one soprano had called him. The three principals of *Fanciulla* were more or less inured to the process, but Caruso couldn't help but wonder how any newcomers in the cast and chorus might take to it.

He wasn't going to get a chance to find out right away. The first rehearsal ended as smoothly as it had begun, with no outbursts and not even a major disagreement. Puccini was pleased with what he'd heard and said so.

Emmy Destinn was both pleased and skeptical. "I don't know how long it will last — but isn't it wonderful?"

Ugo appeared with Caruso's hat and coat. "You see? I make no disturbance at all."

Caruso had sung himself into a state of advanced hunger and Amato had worked up a thirst; they decided to remedy the situation. In the passageway outside the rehearsal hall they collided with a short, plump, pink-faced man who'd obviously been waiting for the rehearsal to end. Caruso started to apologize — but then recognized the man.

"Oh, it's you!" Caruso had blotted the man's name out of his memory. "Every year you ask me, and every year I tell you the same thing. *No!*"

"Why, Mr. Caruso, what a pleasure to see you again!" the pink-faced man said with no trace of uneasiness. "I'm looking forward to *La Fanciulla* — a new Puccini opera! How wonderful. I'm sure you'll be magnificent."

"The answer is still no," the tenor said firmly. "And I do not want you following me around, lying in wait for me — "

"You do me an injustice, sir," the pink-faced man said blandly. "I'm here to see

Mr. Puccini, not you."

"Oh." Caruso felt foolish. He glanced quickly at Amato, who was trying not to laugh. "Well, well, he's still inside." Caruso waved a hand at the rehearsal hall and hurried away.

Amato caught up with him. "Who was that cherubic little man?"

"No cherub, let me assure you. I cannot remember his name— I do not want to remember it!"

"But you know him?"

"Alas, yes. He is a small-time impresario who keeps asking me to let him schedule extra concert appearances for me. I tell him and I tell him, all my singing engagements are arranged by my regular agents— but he does not take no for an answer. For six or seven years he has been pestering me!"

"Hm. He has never asked *me.*"

"Be grateful. Pasquale, do you know what he did? He tried to bribe Martino to persuade me to sign with him! Imagine! He actually tried to bribe my valet!"

Amato glanced back at the other valet trailing after them. "Good thing he did not approach Ugo," he said, his voice lowered.

"Oh, Ugo is all right— he would never

take a bribe." He shot a questioning look at his friend. "You have never liked Ugo, have you? Why not?"

"I don't know," Amato said honestly. "But I don't. He is certainly no Martino, is he? Ah, but that is an unfair comparison. Martino is special."

"How do you mean?"

"Well, for one thing, he is the only man I know who can maintain his dignity while wearing a polka-dot bow tie."

Caruso sent Ugo back to the Knicker-bocker while he and Amato went off to deal with the twin threats of starvation and dehydration.

In mid-November Caruso opened the Metropolitan Opera's new season in a production of Gluck's *Armide*. It was not one of his favorite operas, but the audience loved it. New York audiences loved anything Caruso sang. The tenor sometimes suspected he could walk out on the stage of the Met and sing nursery rhymes and be cheered for it. He tried to keep a sense of perspective about the whole thing.

It wasn't easy. The opening of the opera season signaled the opening of the social season as well; and as usual, Caruso found himself being lionized—another reason he liked New York so much. But invitations to dinners and other social events were also coming from Philadelphia and Boston; much to his regret, Caruso had to turn them down. Until *Fanciulla* premièred, at least. As it was, he barely had time to breathe.

Rehearsals were still progressing smoothly; Toscanini hadn't bitten off a single head yet. The only thing bothering Caruso was that persistent soreness in the throat; it simply would not go away. He'd told young Mario to increase the amount of Dobell's Solution in the spray, but it hadn't helped.

Then they were ready to leave the rehearsal hall and start putting everything together on the stage. The first time singers and orchestra rehearsed together was always exciting, so Caruso made a point of getting to the opera house early.

And found everyone else had too. Puccini and Gatti-Casazza were conferring at the back of the auditorium, with the latter doing all the talking. Toscanini was in the orchestra pit, trying to explain himself in halting English to those American musicians who'd never had the good manners to learn Italian. Emmy Destinn was in the wings, quarreling with her maid. Pasquale Amato was prowling the stage, familiarizing himself with the markings on the floor that laid out the set for the first act — which was to be a western saloon.

Caruso strapped on an imaginary gun and practiced his fast draw.

"Have you talked to Puccini lately?" Amato asked him.

"Not for a few days. Why?"

"Something is bothering him."

Caruso sighed. "Then we will hear about it, you may be sure." When one of his own operas was involved, Puccini could be very high-handed indeed.

"I don't know," Amato said. "He just doesn't seem himself."

Caruso glanced toward the back of the auditorium; both Puccini and Gatti-Casazza were gone. Then he noticed a figure sitting in the fifth or sixth row, someone he'd never seen before. Silver-haired and dignified, the man wore a black suit and a high clerical collar. That made Caruso uneasy; what was the Church going to think of the rough-and-tumble low-life they'd be showing on the stage? "Who is the priest?" he whispered to Amato.

"No priest. He is David Belasco."

Ah, so that was Belasco! The man who'd written and produced *The Girl of the Golden West*. Of course he'd want to see what the operatic stage was doing with his play. "Why does he dress as a priest?"

Amato lifted his shoulders, spread his hands.

"Lady and gentlemen!" Toscanini called from the pit. "We commence to begin, yes?"

The first onstage rehearsal of Giacomo Puccini's Wild West opera began, proceeding in Toscanini's usual start-and-stop manner. Listening offstage, Caruso thought it sounded pretty good, considering how confused things always were at this stage of rehearsal. Soon after Caruso made his entrance he spotted a cigarette glowing at the back of the auditorium: it was Puccini. The composer smoked incessantly during rehearsals, even more than Caruso. But then composers didn't have to sing.

During one of the interruptions, Pasquale Amato was refereeing a mild dispute between Caruso and Emmy Destinn over how a certain passage should be sung when a soft voice spoke behind them. "Excuse me, may I make a suggestion?" The priestly figure of David Belasco had joined them on the stage. "If you could sing to each other instead of to the audience, you will create a much more realistic stage picture."

Caruso was surprised at how short the man was — but his small stature cost him none of his impressive dignity. "If we do not sing to the audience, the voice will be lost upstage," Caruso told him.

Belasco smiled. "Mr. Caruso, you could make yourself heard three blocks away if you wished. Believe me, nothing will be lost if you sing to each other. And a great deal will be gained."

Emmy and Amato exchanged a look, shrugged.

"I realize this is your first time on stage," Belasco went on, "but I have found that establishing good habits early in rehearsal always pays off. Please, won't you try it? Sing to each other."

The three singers agreed to do as he asked, without fully understanding why they'd agreed. Toscanini was making noises in the orchestra pit; Belasco left the stage as quietly as he had come.

The hours spent at the piano with Barthélemy were bearing fruit; Toscanini was interrupting Caruso less and less. The first act of *Fanciulla* drew to a close with a dreamlike repetition of an earlier theme that grew softer and softer—but then burst into flame once more at the very end, finally dying away on an unresolved chord. Like a question, waiting to be answered in Act II.

Caruso sighed with pure pleasure. He loved this opera.

Every day the Maestro allowed them to sing longer and longer without stopping them; Caruso couldn't remember another Toscanini rehearsal that had gone so smoothly. The tenor sprayed his throat every few minutes and started singing full voice.

David Belasco had first come to rehearsal out of curiosity, but somehow he'd managed to take over the stage direction. Gatti-Casazza was delighted and offered Belasco a salary, which he refused. Once Toscanini saw the improvement in the stage action, he was equally delighted and encouraged Belasco at every opportunity. Their new director was trying to create a more true-to-life picture on the stage. The singers had a hard time learning to underplay, the overstated gestures of operatic acting being deeply ingrained in all of them — but they too came to appreciate what Belasco was doing for them.

Only Puccini failed to respond with enthusiasm. It wasn't that he disapproved of Belasco's direction; he just didn't seem to care one way or the other. The composer was abstracted a great deal of the time, his mind elsewhere. The world première of his new opera was coming up in less than two weeks' time, Caruso thought, and his mind was elsewhere!

"You are right, something is wrong," the tenor said to Amato during a break. "He is not really here with us, is he? He turns down my invitations, he does not want to talk. He lets Toscanini make all the decisions. *That* is not our friend Puccini."

Amato ventured a guess. "Do you suppose he is brooding over Elvira and that poor dead girl again? What was her name?"

"Doria. No, I think he is over that. This is something else."

"*Mister* Caruso!" said a feminine voice.

Emmy Destinn's maid had come up to them. She was a big-boned Swedish woman with eyebrows and lashes so pale they were virtually invisible. Her name was Sigrid. "Madame Destinn wants to know if you are *quite* ready?"

"For Emmy, I am always ready," Caruso said expansively. "Is there a thing in particular I am supposed to be ready for?"

"*If* you will remember," Sigrid said sarcastically, "Mr. Belasco wanted you to practice the first-act dancing scene."

Caruso struck his forehead. *"Per dio!* I forget. But I already waltz perfectly — what need is there to practice?"

The woman snickered. "Madame Destinn says you step on her feet."

"I?" Caruso was astonished. "She steps on *my* feet!"

She laughed at him openly. "If you could only admit there is something you cannot do — "

"Sigrid," Amato interposed quickly, "tell Emmy he'll be right there." The Swedish woman turned and left without another word.

"Impossible woman," Caruso grumbled. "She always laughs at me. At me!"

"Ah well. Just laugh back, Rico."

Caruso found Emmy and a relatively free space backstage where they could work on their dance. They practiced the waltz, humming the tune and glaring at each other all the while. But by the time they got the steps worked out, they were friends again.

"Why don't you discharge that Sigrid?" Caruso asked, still smarting a little.

"Why don't you discharge that Ugo?" Emmy countered.

"Why? What has Ugo done?"

"He told Sigrid I need to lose twenty pounds."

"Ugo is crazy. You look wonderful."

"Hmph."

When the day's rehearsal had ended, Caruso wanted to ask Puccini about something. The tenor was nervous; he knew he had no business making the request. He thought he'd found a place in Act II where a cadenza could be inserted.

Cadenzas were the lifeblood of a singer — those passages in a solo piece that allowed the performer to improvise and display his versatility. Unfortunately, the cadenza more properly belonged to the older bel canto operas— which would accommodatingly halt in their action now and then to allow the singers to show off what they could do with a tricky vocal line. That kind of ornamental singing had no place in a verismo opera like *Fanciulla,* with its action and music so carefully integrated, so carefully controlled. But perhaps Puccini would allow *one* cadenza.

Since the composer always watched from the back of the auditorium, Caruso hurried down the aisle to catch him before he left. The auditorium lights were not on, and Caruso could barely make out two figures by the door, talking in low voices. "Puccini? Are you there?"

"Yes? What is it, Caruso?" Puccini asked shortly. "I'm in a hurry."

The composer's tone of voice told Caruso this was not the time to ask for favors, but the tenor plowed on anyway. He'd brought a copy of the score with him. "Here in the second act," Caruso said, pointing to the spot in the score, "such a perfect place for a cadenza! Right after the—"

"A cadenza! Are you out of your mind? Absolutely not!" Puccini was angry. "You should know better than to ask, Caruso."

"Ah, but here it is right! When the—"

"It is wrong, wrong! No cadenza!" Puccini glanced toward the shadowy figure waiting for him. "I must go, I have business."

Caruso sighed. "Not even a small one?"

Puccini shook his head in irritation and turned away.

Pity, Caruso thought sadly. A *little* cadenza wouldn't hurt.

Puccini was opening the auditorium door; light from the lobby spilled in, and for the first time Caruso could see the man who'd been waiting for the composer. He was surprised; it was the pudgy pink-faced impresario who'd been badgering Caruso for years to sign with him. The man who'd tried to bribe Martino. Now what in the world was Puccini doing with a man like that?

The door swung to and Caruso was alone in the dark. Surely Puccini must know what kind of man the impresario was. He wasn't even a real impresario; he was just one of that group of people who lived on the fringe of the music world, leeching off whatever celebrities they could attach themselves to. They had no talents of their own and they did no honest work. They spent their lives looking for a piece of somebody else's pie.

And here was Puccini, in such a hurry to go off with that pink-faced leech. Belatedly it occurred to Caruso that the composer might *not* know what kind of man the so-called impresario was. If that was the case, then clearly it was Caruso's duty to warn him.

He pushed through the auditorium door; the lobby of the Fortieth Street entrance was empty except for one lone birdlike figure. It was Toscanini, concentrating intently on something he held in his hand and totally unaware of Caruso's presence.

"Maestro!" the tenor called. "Do you see Puccini and another man just now? Do you know where they go?"

Toscanini started guiltily and thrust whatever he was holding into his pocket. "Ah . . . Caruso! Ah, what did you say? Puccini . . . I do not know, they, ah . . ." Abruptly his manner changed; he became stern and professorial. "No partying tonight, Caruso! You need your rest. Leave the ladies alone. Do you understand?" He whirled on his heel and was gone.

Caruso stared after him in astonishment. Now what in the name of heaven was *that* all about?

THREE

My dear Puccini,

    It is with great reluctance that I must insist you call upon me today in my apartment at the Hotel Knickerbocker. If you do not come today, I refuse to attend the Fanciulla rehearsal. More than that, I will never sing the role if you do not come.

    I am certain you realize what a great personal sacrifice such a position costs me, but you leave me no choice. You will not talk to me on the telephone and you do not answer my letters. The last time I called on you, you shut the door in my face. So you see, only the deepest desperation could drive me to issue such an ultimatum. I refuse to sing if you do not come.

I expect to see you immediately without fail. I accept no excuses.

Your loving friend,
E. Caruso

Caruso read the letter over in distaste; such a *bullying* thing to write! He'd written it in what Pasquale Amato said was his "angry" handwriting— large, irregularly shaped letters with heavy dots and dashes. His "polite" handwriting, as Amato called it, was uniform in size and tastefully ornamented with numerous little curlicues. But by heaven he *was* angry, and this was no time to be polite.

"What do you think?" Caruso asked Martino, who was reading over his shoulder.

"A very strong, persuasive letter," the valet said approvingly. "Perhaps if you underlined the word 'never'. . . ?"

Caruso dipped his pen in the inkwell and drew a heavy black line under "never."

"Yes, that is better," Martino nodded. "That should get him here."

Caruso blotted the letter and folded it carefully into an envelope. "Ugo, I want you to take this to Puccini. Do not leave it with the hotel clerk—hand it to Puccini personally."

"I will take it, Rico," Martino said. "I must go out anyway, to buy supplies."

Ugo said, "Be sure you bring back the receipts."

"You say that every time I go out," Martino answered with a touch of exasperation. "Have I ever forgotten to bring back the receipts?"

"No. But that does not mean you will never forget." Ugo was the bookkeeper in Caruso's traveling household, a job that by rights should have been Martino's. But with all his various abilities, the one thing Martino could not do was add and subtract. Not with any reasonable degree of reliability, unfortunately.

When Martino had left, Caruso told Ugo to prepare some wine and sat down to wait.

Forty minutes later, Puccini was there —breathing fire. "What do you mean, you *refuse* to sing? You signed a contract! Caruso, how dare you threaten me! You—"

"Let me explain, let me explain!" Caruso felt terrible; he was beginning to wish he hadn't started this. "There is a reason—"

"Do I not have enough trouble without

your threats? Elvira pours out her anger in long, long letters and Toscanini will never have *Fanciulla* ready in time and my new valet has run away! And now you tell me— "

"*Fanciulla* will be ready in plenty of time," Caruso soothed. "And your new valet is probably just lost again."

"No, no, he took all his clothes— and even some of mine! He has run away!" Puccini sank down into a chair. "Obviously he applied for the job only to get passage to America. He never had any intention of staying with me."

Caruso tsk-tsked and made other appropriate noises until he finally got the composer calmed down enough to listen. "Puccini, I know something else is wrong — something is terribly wrong. I want you to tell me about it. Perhaps I can help!"

"What are you talking about?" Puccini snapped. "Nothing else is wrong! Isn't that enough?"

Caruso swallowed and stuck out his chin. "I do not believe you."

"Will you mind your own business? How dare you pry into my life! I tell you nothing is wrong."

"If nothing is wrong, then why are you

not enjoying yourself?" Irrefutable logic, from Caruso's point of view. "Just think, Puccini. This should be a joyous time for you, seeing all the parts of your new opera come together. But you are listless, distracted—you seem indifferent to what is happening. How can you not care what happens to *Fanciulla?* Something is terribly wrong. Everyone can see it."

The composer said nothing.

"Puccini," Caruso said with a certain amount of unrehearsed bravado, "I am not going to let you go until you tell me what is bothering you. You and I, we will spend the rest of our lives right here together in this room—unless you tell me. I do not joke. You *will* tell me."

Puccini stared at him a long time without speaking. His face began to change; he seemed to be aging even as Caruso watched. Then the composer gave a shudder and dropped his face into his hands.

Alarmed, Caruso jumped to his feet. "What is it? What distresses you so?"

Slowly the composer lifted a grief-stricken face from his hands; Caruso had never seen such a tortured look offstage in his life. Puccini had to swallow twice before he could speak. "Do you know a man named Luigi Davila?"

Davila, Davila . . . ah, *Davila!* Yes, yes—Davila was the pink-faced impresario whose name Caruso had managed to forget. The man with whom Puccini had left the Metropolitan Opera House. Luigi Davila. "I do know him, alas—I wish I did not! The man is a pest."

"He is more than a pest," Puccini said. "He's a blackmailer. I am being blackmailed, Caruso. Luigi Davila is blackmailing me."

"Oh, my dear friend!" Caruso's heart melted in sympathy. "What a terrible, terrible thing!" Blackmail! The tenor wandered around the room, waving his arms in frustration. "My dear Puccini—I ache for you!" Because he couldn't think what else to do, he yelled to Ugo to bring the wine.

Puccini was trembling all over. "It never stops. One misfortune after another."

Ugo came in with the wine, took one look at Puccini, and asked if he should go for a doctor.

"No, no," Caruso said, "just give him some wine. Quickly."

Ugo poured them each a glass of wine, but the composer's hand was so shaky the valet had to help him lift the glass to his mouth. "Is there something I can get you?" he asked solicitously. Puccini shook his head.

Caruso tossed off his wine and held the glass out for more. He seated himself opposite Puccini and took a deep breath. "Now then. Tell me the whole thing."

"This, this *Davila*"— Puccini made the name sound obscene— "this Davila says he has evidence that will send Elvira to prison for the rest of her life."

Elvira again! "What has she done now?"

"Nothing! It is that same tragic affair in Torre del Lago!"

"The servant girl Doria?"

Puccini nodded. "Davila says she didn't poison herself. He says she was murdered, and it was Elvira who murdered her!" Both Caruso and Ugo were staring at him open-mouthed. "Neither Elvira nor I was in Torre del Lago when Doria swallowed the poison," Puccini went on.

"But if you were not there . . . ?"

Puccini didn't seem to hear. "Caruso, do you know it took her five days to die? *Five days.* All that agony . . . the suffering she must have gone through! And the poor girl never did harm to anyone."

Ugo filled the composer's wineglass and patted him sympathetically on the shoulder.

Caruso tried again. "How could Elvira murder the girl if she was not there?"

"Davila says she did not administer the poison herself— she is supposed to have hired someone to do it for her. Davila says he has letters she wrote arranging the whole thing."

"You have seen these letters?"

"He showed me one. Elvira did not write that letter, Caruso, no question of it. But it looks just enough *like* her handwriting that it might succeed in deceiving people who are not so familiar with her writing as I am. But it is *not* her writing. Besides, Elvira is not stupid— she would never put something like that down on paper. And then sign her full name? Preposterous. The letters are forged, and Davila knows I know they are forged. But they could still convict Elvira! He has me. I cannot risk even the accusation. They convicted her once before, in Torre del Lago."

"But that was for defamation, not murder!"

"It makes no difference. You know how I

got Elvira out of it — by paying off Doria's family? The good people of Torre del Lago feel cheated. They would love nothing more than a second chance at my wife."

Caruso jumped up again and started pacing the floor. He had trouble believing what was happening. And all because of that Luigi Davila! What kind of worm would take advantage of such a terrible tragedy to extort money from a man? How low, how vile! What to do, what to do? "Do you trust him to keep quiet if you pay him off?" he asked Puccini.

"He does not want to be paid *off*. He wants to be paid, and paid, and paid. He made it quite clear I am to see he lives in comfort for the rest of his days. Luigi Davila is a vampire — he will suck me dry."

Wide-eyed, Ugo poured himself a glass of wine and drank it down fast.

"This you cannot agree to," Caruso said in dismay. "Spend the rest of your life supporting that . . . that *leech*. Impossible."

"But what else can I do?" Puccini groaned. "I cannot let Elvira go to prison for a crime she didn't commit — she might even be hanged!"

"Does she know anything about this?"

"No, and you are not to tell her, Caruso."

"Of course not, of course not. But we must think of what to do!"

"I've thought and I've thought, but there is nothing."

They mulled it over for a while, getting nowhere, not able to think of any possible line of action.

"Once again you have gotten me to talk, Caruso," Puccini smiled sadly. "And I must tell you, I am grateful. I did want to tell somebody— it is a terrible burden to bear alone. But Caruso, you must mention this to no one else— no one at all."

"I say nothing, I give you my word." Then they both remembered the third man in the room.

Ugo held up his hands, palms outward. "I do not repeat one word of what I hear. I promise. I tell no one."

"Not even Martino and Mario," Caruso ordered.

"Especially not Martino and Mario," Ugo agreed. "Martino talks too much, and Mario does not talk enough."

Caruso didn't quite follow that, but decided this wasn't the time to pursue it. A little later Puccini left, after promising to keep Caruso informed. The tenor continued his pacing, thinking.

"Ugo — you know this Luigi Davila, don't you?"

"I am not sure."

"You were there once or twice when he wanted me to sign a contract — oh, you know, he is the one who tried to bribe Martino! Do you remember him?"

Ugo squinted his eyes. "Pink and fat?"

"That's the one! Ugo, I want you to find out where he lives. Or where his office is — if he has an office."

"How do I do that?"

Caruso glared at him; he hadn't thought that far ahead. "Eh, you can try asking at the opera house — Mr. Gatti knows everyone. Or — I know! — booking offices! Some of the other agents must surely know him."

Ugo's face lit up. "That is a good idea, Rico! I will go right now." He hurried off to get his hat and coat.

Caruso continued his pacing and heard Ugo leave. Poor Puccini! How could any man bear it? He did not deserve this.

The tenor was jittery, edgy. He still had a rehearsal to get through today, and he was in no condition to concentrate on singing.

He needed something to relax him. "Mario!"

He had to call only once; the youngest of his three valets was there, waiting quietly to hear what his employer wanted.

"I will have my massage now, Mario. Immediately!"

The young man didn't so much as blink at this outrageous change in routine. Mario always gave Caruso a rubdown after rehearsals, when the tenor was tense and wound up. He must have wondered why Caruso wanted a massage now, *before* going to the opera house. When Caruso was ready, Mario started slapping scented oil on his back.

"Mario, what does one do with a blackmailer?" Caruso asked.

"One goes to the police, signore."

"Hm. But what if going to the police causes harm? Harm to innocent people?"

"One goes anyway. Better the risk of harm than putting one's life into the hands of a blackmailer."

Caruso shook his head and dropped the subject. He'd forgotten the absoluteness of youth—this is right, that is wrong. "Mario, that suit you are wearing is starting to look frayed. You have been wearing it how long?"

Mario thought back. "Only two and three-fourths years." Caruso took a moment to figure out that three-fourths of a year was nine months. "Go get yourself a new one— have the bill sent to me."

"*Grazie, signore, grazie!*" Mario beat a happy tattoo on the tenor's back.

Caruso grunted and dismissed Mario's sartorial problem from his mind. There had to be something he could do to help Puccini. There *had* to be.

New York barbershops were, to Enrico Caruso's way of thinking, one of the seven wonders of the modern world. They were not just for haircuts and shaves— oh no! There one could also be perfumed, powdered, manicured, pedicured, steamed, and massaged. One could buy toilet articles there, or ease sore muscles by lying under a heat lamp. Or one could clear congested nasal passages by breathing a specially prepared sulpha vapor. And every barbershop in Manhattan boasted its own particular cure for hangover.

But what Caruso liked most about the better barbershops were their bathtubs.

Huge, commodious things that were far more comfortable than the tub he used at the hotel. Plus rows and rows of bottled scent for the water: lilac, mimosa, sandalwood, musk rose, lavender, blue hyacinth, verbena, hibiscus, wisteria, violet, birch leaf, chinaberry, honeysuckle — the tenor wanted to try them all. (Except gardenia; Caruso never used gardenia. He couldn't stand the soprano the scent was named after.) Caruso could soak in the barbershop bath for hours if he wished, the attendants constantly making sure the water stayed at the temperature he liked. New York barbershops were, in short, havens of repose and comfort for tired businessmen and distraught opera singers.

Mario's massage had gotten him through the rehearsal well enough; but at the end of the day Caruso felt the need to soak and steam — and talk. He liked the camaraderie of the barbershops, but that wasn't the kind of talk he wanted this time. He persuaded Pasquale Amato to go with him to Tonio's on Seventh Avenue, where he asked for a private room with two tubs.

Once he and Amato were installed in their tubs, Caruso told the attendants not to come in until he rang for them. Then he proceeded to tell Amato everything he had earlier in the day promised Puccini he would never reveal to anyone.

Amato swore. "No wonder he has been distracted. How can a man concentrate on work with something like that hanging over his head?"

Caruso cast a quick glance around the small bathroom to make sure no one had sneaked in when he wasn't looking. "Do you know what I think it is?" He lowered his voice conspiratorially. "I think it is the Black Hand!"

"Ah, not again!"

"Why not again? Because they fail to extort money from me? That does not mean they are going to stop! The Black Hand *never* stops."

"Rico, that is the first thing *you* think of, naturally enough. But to assume this man who is blackmailing Puccini — "

"It *is* the Black Hand, I feel it!" Caruso was sweating, and not just from the heat of the bath. The last time he'd been in New York, the Black Hand had threatened his life. The price for his safety had been fifteen thousand dollars, to be delivered to an address in Brooklyn. Caruso had summoned the police, who'd provided the terrified tenor with an armed guard, even in the opera house. Then Martino had taken a dummy package to the Brooklyn address, where police were watching. Two men were captured; a third escaped. That had all been earlier in the year, in February, but Caruso still couldn't think about it without breaking into a sweat.

Amato was watching his friend carefully. "Rico, are you still afraid of them?"

"Yes," Caruso admitted without hesitation. "What of reprisals? One of the men escaped, remember. And they must have friends." Caruso scowled. "And now they are after Puccini."

"Do not be so sure of that," the baritone mused. "The Black Hand is made up of thugs and hoodlums, Rico. I can believe they'd go to Puccini and threaten to break his arms or put out his eyes if he doesn't pay them off— that is their style. No finesse. But think a moment. Can you really see these thugs going to the trouble of locating a sample of Elvira Puccini's handwriting, and then sitting down and forging those letters? And doing a good enough job of it that most people would be fooled? Rico, a lot of those Black Handers cannot even read and write! This is just not their kind of crime. It is too calculated."

A glimmer of hope appeared in Caruso's face. "Do you really think so?"

"I really think so. In fact, I am willing to lay a small wager that Puccini's blackmailer is one man acting on his own. You did say the man is a small-time impresario, did you not? Does that sound like the Black Hand to you?"

Caruso splashed his tub water happily; he was willing to be convinced. "So we have only one man to worry about. But what do I do? I sent Ugo to find out his address— I think I may sign a contract with Luigi Davila after all. A few extra concerts will not hurt me. I just might do it."

"*Cielo!* Why?"

"Well, perhaps if that nasty pink man can make a little success, be a real impresario . . . you see? If he makes money from me, legitimately— he may leave Puccini alone!"

Amato threw back his head and laughed. "Sometimes you can be so wonderfully innocent, Rico! That is not the answer. Don't you see, then he would just have his

68

hooks into both of you. A man like that has no honor. It is a generous impulse, Rico, but a bad idea. I suggest you forget it."

Caruso agreed readily, since he hadn't thought too much of the idea in the first place. "By the way, you understand you are to repeat all this to no one," he cautioned belatedly. "If anyone asks, you do not know anything about it. I gave Puccini my solemn word I do not tell his secret. But I am at my wit's end trying to figure out how to help. You always know what to do, Pasquale. Suggest something."

Amato was silent a moment. Then: "You are asking my advice?"

"Yes, I am asking your advice."

"Then my advice is to stay out of it. You coerced Puccini into revealing his secret in the first place, yes? And if you start meddling you will just make things worse. Rico, old friend, mind your own business."

"How can I do that?" Caruso protested. "When a friend needs help—"

"But since we both know you have never minded your own business in your life," Amato went on smoothly, "my *second* piece of advice is to find this black-mailer and confront him yourself. Find this Luigi . . . ?"

"Davila."

"Davila, yes. Go to him and tell him you know what he is doing. If he thinks other people know about it, he just might back down. No man wants to be known as a blackmailer. Too risky."

Caruso sat up straight in his tub. "You think that will work?"

"It might. It will depend on how easily intimidated this man Davila is."

"Will you go with me?"

"How can I?" Amato blew soapsuds in Caruso's direction. "I do not even know about this, remember? And Rico— I still think my first advice is the best. Don't meddle in it."

Caruso swooshed the water with his toes, thinking. "Pasquale— if our positions were reversed, what would you do? Would *you* stay out of it? Or would you try to help?"

Amato was silent for so long that Caruso began to think he'd fallen asleep. Then the baritone sighed, musically. "I'd try to help."

Caruso leaned back in the tub and smiled. It was the answer he wanted.

FOUR

THE FOLLOWING DAY Caruso was excused from the *Fanciulla* rehearsal. He was singing *Pagliacci* that night, and Toscanini had agreed to rehearse around him, just this once. The conductor knew how much preparation a heavy tragic role like *Pagliacci* demanded of a singer.

That was another mystery Caruso had to contend with. Why was Toscanini being so understanding? This was unnatural behavior, to say the least.

It took some doing for Caruso to get himself into the proper frame of mind for the heavier operatic roles. His usual procedure was to spend most of the day lying down. He would vocalize very little, and then always in long, sustained phrases, building up gradually until it was time to go

71

to the opera house. By then he would be in the initial stages of a first-class, grade-A *panic*.

Enrico Caruso suffered from stage fright. *Terrible* stage fright; it had been with him all his life and showed no sign of going away. Over the years it had fallen to his accompanist Barthélemy to nurse the tenor through these pre-performance jitters, to supply him with headache medicine and throat spray and analgesic powders and generally soothe and encourage him any way he could. Once Caruso stepped out on the stage, he was all right; but that period right before a performance began was hell for everybody.

So it was to everyone's benefit if the day preceding an evening performance could be spent calmly. Caruso tried lying down and blanking his mind, but this time the trick didn't work. Ugo had turned up an address for Luigi Davila, and facing the blackmailer was all Caruso could think of. He found, to his distress, that he didn't want to do it.

When Davila had been just an annoying little man trying to hitch a free ride on Caruso's coattails, the tenor had known how to respond to him. But now that

Caruso was aware Davila was a blackmailer, or a would-be blackmailer— well, that made a difference. One did not speak to blackmailers the same way one spoke to ordinary pests.

To get his mind off the matter, Caruso went to his desk to read some of his mail. Everyone in the household took turns with the mail; and sometimes Caruso had to ask friends to come in and help, there was so much of it. Some of it came to the hotel, but most was sent to the Metropolitan Opera. A New York postal clerk had once told Caruso that he received as much mail as an entire small town.

The first letter he picked up followed a common pattern.

> *Dear Cousin Enrico,*
> *You may not remember me from our early days in Naples, as I was only a child when you left. I have been living in the United States of America for three years now and have fallen upon hard times. . . .*

The letter went on to ask for a small stake to start a coal-and-wood business in Ohio and was signed *Federico Caruso.*

It was amazing the number of Carusos that had sprung up in the world over the past few years. True, "Caruso" was a very common name, but no man alive ever had as many relatives as the number that now claimed kinship to *the* Caruso. Federico Caruso, for instance — the tenor had never heard of him. For all he knew, Federico might be a cousin at that. The amount of money the man asked for was modest, so Caruso wrote him out a check.

"Rico!" Ugo said reprovingly, looking over the tenor's shoulder. "You must stop giving so much money away! Who is this 'Federico Caruso'? Another long-lost relative, undoubtedly?"

"Well, well, perhaps."

Ugo snorted. *"Anybody* can ask you for money and get it! What do you know of this Federico? He could be a liar and a thief! He could beat his wife and children!"

Caruso waved his arm in the air, inadvertently sprinkling Ugo with ink. "How am I to know which ones are deserving? They cannot *all* be liars!"

Ugo threw up his arms in disgust and stormed away. Caruso returned to his mail;

they had had this argument before. Ugo was downright stingy with Caruso's money; keeping the accounts had given him a proprietary interest in it, Caruso supposed.

But even as he went on reading the mail, his thoughts kept returning to Puccini and Luigi Davila. Finally he pushed the mail away in irritation; concentration was impossible. He took out his sketch pad and tried a few drawings but couldn't get the lines to go right. He slammed the pad shut and was annoyed that it didn't make more noise.

Caruso sat and twiddled his thumbs for a few moments. Then he thought of his watches—ah yes, he would play with his watches! He hurried into another room and started taking small black boxes out of a bureau drawer. Caruso had only recently begun collecting the eighteenth-century enameled gold timepieces, but already he had enough of them to make an impressive display. The tenor loved their look and their touch; he loved the heavy feel of them in his hand. But today the watches failed to work their usual magic; Caruso was just handling them without seeing their beauty. He put the boxes back in the drawer.

The Hotel Knickerbocker apartment had

eight rooms; the times Caruso had stayed there before, the place had been ample enough. But today the rooms seemed to be shrinking in on him. He prowled all eight of them, looking for something, anything to distract him. Barthélemy was out, running some personal errand. Ugo was seated at a table working on the accounts, still grumbling over what he considered Caruso's excessive open-handedness. Mario had turned invisible, as he always did when he was not needed. Martino was sewing a button on a coat.

Caruso sat down and watched Ugo and Martino work. He didn't feel like reading or playing cards. A trace of morning hoarseness still remained in his throat, so it was too early to start vocalizing. He should lie down and rest. He jumped up and sprayed the room with perfume.

"Is something wrong, Rico?" Martino asked. "Shouldn't you be resting?"

Suddenly Caruso felt that if he didn't get out of that apartment he would suffocate. "Martino! Bring me my coat and hat. I am going out!"

"To distribute alms among the poor, no doubt," Ugo muttered from his table.

Martino brought Caruso his hat and fur-collared coat, his gloves and cane. "Where are you going, Rico?" The same question he asked every time Caruso left the apartment. Like a mother hen checking up on one of her chicks.

"I am going to see my tailor," Caruso lied.

"You do not wish him to come here? Shall I call him on the telephone?"

"No, no, this time I go to him. I am going to buy a new suit and a new pair of shoes," he improvised.

"Rico," Martino laughed, "you already have *eighty* pairs of shoes!"

"Eighty?"

"And fifty suits."

"Fifty!"

Ugo, low: "All two sizes too small."

"And," Martino finished with a flourish, "a dozen hats!"

Caruso's eyes grew large. *"Per dio!* It is a new *hat* that I need!"

Out he marched.

Caruso stepped off the streetcar at the corner of Third Avenue and Fourteenth Street and took a few moments to get his bearings. East Fourteenth Street — once the center of New York's entertainment world until the theatres had started moving uptown, first to Herald Square and then to Times Square. Now the street had a run-down, faded-glory look to it, a roosting place for also-rans and left-behinds, people like Luigi Davila who'd never really been part of the mainstream at all.

The tenor headed west on Fourteenth. He passed imposing Tammany Hall, the west wing of which was given over to Tony Pastor's variety theatre. American vaudeville had been born in that little theatre; but by this time next year both the vaudeville house and the rest of Tammany would be gone. A demolition notice posted on the wall told Caruso the new Consolidated Gas Company Building would be going up in their place.

Next door to doomed Tammany Hall stood the still-struggling Academy of Music. Once Manhattan's leading opera house, the Academy had switched to straight drama some twenty years hack when the newer, more splendiferous Metropolitan had stolen its audience — deliberately. Caruso didn't know it, but David Belasco's first New York hit had been staged at the Academy, a melodrama called *The Girl I Left Behind Me.* Now a billboard heralded the virtues of the theatre's current production, the American Civil War drama *Shenandoah.*

Caruso could glimpse the façade of Steinway Hall a little farther along East Fourteenth, just past Irving Place. A handsome building with pillars in front, Steinway Hall used to be the classical music center of the country. Used to be. Everything about this neighborhood was used-to-be. Feeling depressed, the tenor turned into Irving Place.

And was not encouraged by what he saw. Two German-language theatres had managed to hang on, and a second-story window sign in a grubby-looking building proclaimed the existence of a school of elocution and dramatic art. But Irving Place had been invaded by a rash of small stores, most with living quarters over them and all of them run-down and neglected. George Wlasenko, Banner Painter. O'Reilly's Straw Goods and Giambelli's Music Publishing, sharing the same building. Dr. Cohen, Painless Dentistry. Certainly a mixed neighborhood, in more ways than one.

Caruso passed a Finnish cabinetmaker's

shop and came to the number he was looking for. It was a three-story brown building, every bit as shabby as its neighbors. Not a brownstone, just . . . brown. He didn't want to go in. But he'd never be able to concentrate on that night's performance if he failed to confront Davila. A woman in the street recognized the tenor and tried to tell him about her out-of-work husband and her sick mother and the overdue rent and this nagging pain she had in her back; Caruso was so absorbed he didn't even hear her. He climbed the brown building's six steps without answering, thus losing a fan forever.

The door of the brown building had a cracked glass panel; inside, the place even smelled brown. The tiny entryway was dingy and contained no directory that Caruso could see. He opened a door marked JOS. PEARS, WATCHMAKER and asked the man inside where Luigi Davila's office was. Second floor.

Caruso carefully picked his way up the dark, narrow stairs, as leery of dirt as of tripping and falling. The first door he came to on the second floor bore the legend DAVILA CONCERT BUREAU. Caruso stood for a moment or two in front of the door rehearsing what he was going to say. When he was ready, he tried the door; it opened to his touch.

The "concert bureau" consisted of one scantily furnished office room—a battered desk, a couple of chairs, a lamp, and three wooden apple crates stacked on top of one another in lieu of a filing cabinet. Another room was curtained off at the back. The office was cold; the small gas heater was not turned on. "Davila!" Caruso called out. "Are you here?"

There was no answer. But the door had been unlocked; surely no one would go away and leave a door unlocked in a neighborhood like this one. Perhaps in the back room?

He pushed aside the separating curtain —and hastily withdrew when he saw the back room was Davila's private living quarters, and Davila himself was lying on the floor. He was torn between calling out again and leaving when it occurred to him to wonder why Davila was on the *floor*. And he'd only assumed it was the man he'd come to see; he hadn't really looked at the face. Cautiously he opened the curtain again.

It was Luigi Davila. And he *was* lying on the floor. With a long-handled knife protruding from his side, a pool of blood discoloring the linoleum on the floor.

Caruso had never moved so fast in his life. He stumbled down the dark stairway without thought of danger or dirt. He burst into the room of Jos. ·Pears, Watchmaker, his eyes popping and his arms waving. "Gack gack gack gack gack gack!" he croaked, making stabbing motions toward the ceiling with both forefingers. Alarmed, the watchmaker snatched up a tiny tool to defend himself.

No help there. Caruso rushed out into the street and grabbed the lapels of the first man he saw. "Gack gack gack gack!" he informed the man earnestly. He was sweating now, fear pouring out of every pore.

"Take yer hands off me, yuh looney!" the man snarled unsympathetically. Caruso let go of him and started croaking at two passing women. They screamed and ran away.

"*Polizia!*" Caruso was finally able to shout. "*Commissariato! Uno poliziotto!*" He seemed to have forgotten all his English.

A small crowd was beginning to gather,

attracted by the sight of a well-dressed stranger going noisily bonkers in their midst. Try as he might, the tenor could not make a single one of them understand. "Luigi Davila!" Caruso cried, frantically pointing to the second floor of the building. *"È morto!"* Wouldn't you know, he thought in despair, never an Italian anywhere when you needed one!

A small boy tugged at his sleeve. "Ain't you feeling right, Mister? I'll fetch a doctor fer a nickel."

Tears running down his cheeks, Caruso lowered himself shakily to the steps of the building. The watchmaker was in the doorway, cautiously peeking out. Caruso made his hands into fists and beat his knees in frustration. The crowd energetically discussed Caruso's condition among themselves.

"Here, now, what's all this?" At the sound of the commanding voice Caruso looked up to see an enormous policeman astride a massive horse. "What's going on here?"

"It's Enrico Caruso," someone said. "I think he's having a fit."

The policeman dismounted and tied his horse to a lamppost. "Enrico Caruso, is it?"

He came over to the steps and bent down until his face was level with the tenor's. "What's the trouble, Mr. Caruso?"

Caruso swallowed, took a deep breath, and said in perfectly clear English: "A man named Luigi Davila has been murdered. He is in his rooms on the second floor."

A gasp ran through the crowd. "Poor man," a woman's voice murmured, and Caruso wondered whether she meant Davila or himself; they all thought he was crazy.

"Murdered, you say?" The policeman stood up straight. "Well, now, let's go up and have a look, shall we?"

Caruso shuddered. "No, thank you, I have already had a look. You go. Second floor." Weakly he pointed upward, to show the policeman what direction the second floor was in.

The policeman considered a moment and then said, "All right, you stay here. I'll go see. What was that name again?"

Caruso told him and the policeman went into the building. The tenor lowered his head into his hands, letting the tension start to drain out now that Authority had arrived.

The policeman's thundering footsteps sounded on the stairs behind him; then the piercing shriek of a police whistle hurt his ears. Soon other policemen were there, the crowd of gawkers grew larger, and Enrico Caruso found himself being marched off to a police station.

"Now tell me why you went to see this Luigi Davila, Mr. Caruso."

"I have already told you why," Caruso said in exasperation. "Fourteen times I have told you! Maybe fifteen!"

"So tell me again. Why did you go see him?"

"I want to talk to him about arranging a concert tour for me." When Caruso had first arrived at the station house, he'd been kept waiting for over an hour before anyone got around to questioning him. He'd sat there looking at the high ceilings and the over-sized dirty windows and he'd had time to think. It had gradually dawned on him that whoever killed Luigi Davila had done Giacomo Puccini an enormous favor. Puccini was free now; his life was no longer in the hands of an unscrupulous black-mailer. No one need ever know— so long as Caruso didn't make a mistake and let it slip out why he had really gone to see Davila.

"A concert tour. Mr. Caruso, do you expect me to believe that? You are a big star. Luigi Davila was a penny-ante operator. Why would you switch from your regular agents to the likes of him?"

"No, no, you misunderstand! I am not changing agents. Davila was going to arrange *additional* engagements for me. Little extras, you see."

Caruso knew his interrogator; the man's name was O'Halloran and he was a New York Detective Bureau lieutenant. He had been one of the men responsible for capturing two of the Black Hand members who had threatened the tenor's life earlier in the year. O'Halloran was a lanky, second-generation Irishman who thought John McCormack was the greatest tenor who ever lived. Caruso had never seen the police detective without a derby perched on his head, not even indoors.

"Lieutenant O'Halloran, how much longer do you keep me here?" Caruso asked. "I sing *Pagliacci* tonight. I must prepare." He was getting worried; he'd been at the station house all afternoon. He'd done no vocalizing, he wanted a bath, his stomach was growling, and he was out of cigarettes. And it was almost time to go to the opera house.

"Just a little longer," the police detective said. "Now tell me—"

"At least let Mr. Gatti know where I am."

"Who?"

"Giulio Gatti-Casazza. The general manager of the Metropolitan Opera."

"That's right, I met him—that last time. Well, I suppose we can do that." There was no telephone in the office they were using, so O'Halloran left the room to make the call. He came back immediately and the questioning resumed.

Not more than twenty minutes later Gatti-Casazza rushed in—followed, Caruso was happy to see, by Barthélemy. "Lieutenant O'Halloran!" Gatti-Casazza roared. "What are you doing? Why are you keeping Mr. Caruso here? I demand you release him immediately!"

"Mr. Gatti," Caruso sighed in relief.

"Release him?" O'Halloran said. "He's not under arrest, sir. He is helping us with our inquiries."

"Oh, is that what you call it? Helping you with your inquiries?"

Caruso's accompanist was obviously awed at finding himself inside a bastion of law enforcement. "We were so worried about you, Rico," Barthélemy said. "Martino said you went out to buy a hat."

"Mr. Gatti-Casazza," O'Halloran said, mangling the pronunciation, "it was Mr. Caruso here who discovered the body. We have to ask him questions."

"But surely this can wait until tomorrow," Gatti-Casazza said in a frantic tone of voice. "Mr. Caruso has a performance tonight. The house is sold out. He *must* sing. You have got to let him go!"

While Gatti-Casazza worked on Lieutenant O'Halloran, Barthélemy started his usual chore of calming Caruso down before a performance—a bigger job than usual this time, as the events of the day had not exactly contributed to a sense of composure. The general manager continued arguing with O'Halloran until the police detective finally agreed to let the tenor go to the opera house. "I think I'll tag along," O'Halloran said.

"Why? Do you think I am going to run away?" Caruso asked indignantly.

"Now, Rico, he meant nothing by that," Barthélemy soothed. "It is his job."

"Is it his job to treat me like a criminal?"

Caruso was too wound up by now to be stopped. "All afternoon he keeps me here — asking questions, questions, questions! Do you think I killed Luigi Davila? Do you?"

"Now, Mr. Caruso, I didn't say that."

"Ha! You do not have to say it! Do you think I plunge a knife into his side and then run down to the street to tell everybody about it? Is that what you think?"

"We know it didn't happen like that," O'Halloran said carefully. "The coroner's physician says he's been dead since yesterday."

"Oh." Caruso thought that over and decided it meant he was in the clear. "Well, then, why are we still here? Let us be on our way!"

At the opera house a couple of dozen concerned men and women swarmed over Caruso the minute he entered; word had spread fast. Gatti-Casazza disappeared backstage, exhorting everyone to concentrate only on the performance that was due to begin shortly. O'Halloran followed Caruso and Barthélemy up the stairs to the tenor's dressing room.

Martino was there, laying out the clown make-up. "Rico, are you all right? We were so worried—"

"Yes, yes, I mean no, I mean where is the throat spray?"

O'Halloran lounged in the doorway listening to Caruso warm up as he got into costume and make-up. The tenor was jumpy and high-strung and yelling at Martino and Barthélemy every few seconds. The man was a nervous wreck; O'Halloran didn't see how he could possibly get through a complete performance. The detective began to feel a little guilty.

Finally Martino and Barthélemy had Caruso ready and the three of them hurried down the stairs, O'Halloran trailing. Again Caruso was surrounded by people, everyone jabbering away in Italian. O'Halloran didn't know the language, but it was clear all those people were concerned about their tenor — they were trying to help.

A sudden silence fell. Out in front of the closed curtain, the baritone was singing the Prologue. O'Halloran could feel the tension backstage; he didn't know whether it arose from Caruso's involvement in a murder or whether that tension was normal for the opera house. One thing he was sure of, though; and that was that Enrico Caruso was *loved*. All the time the tenor was waiting to make his entrance, singers and stage-hands alike kept coming up to him, patting him on the shoulder, trying to reassure him. O'Halloran was impressed in spite of himself.

The curtains opened. Shortly thereafter Caruso made his entrance, and that famous golden voice suddenly filled the opera house. O'Halloran worked his way around the obstacle course backstage, trying to stay out of the way. The opera moved along like an electric charge. Caruso brought down the house with *Vesti la giubba* and then hurried off the stage to make a costume change. This time O'Halloran didn't follow him up to the dressing room; it was obvious the tenor had no intention of taking it on the lam.

O'Halloran made his way over to the other side of the stage; Gatti-Casazza was there, watching from the wings. Then Caruso was on the stage again, wearing his clown costume and sweating heavily and singing his heart out. By then O'Halloran was feeling quite bad about having detained the tenor so long at the station house.

"Mr. Gatti-Casazza," he said in an attempt

to atone, "I'm sorry about that unpleasant business this afternoon. I didn't mean to make things difficult for Mr. Caruso. It was just—"

"What are you talking about?" Gatti-Casazza interrupted happily. "Tonight is the greatest *Pagliacci* he has ever sung!"

The audience agreed. Caruso took nineteen curtain calls.

FIVE

Caruso awoke the next morning feeling marvelous.

And why not? He'd scored a triumph the night before—his best *Pagliacci* ever. The audience had gone wild. And that ugly scene he'd walked in on yesterday afternoon had turned out to have a happy ending; the great Puccini was no longer in the grip of a blackmailer. And that detective lieutenant, O'Halloran, had even let him know—in a roundabout way—that he did not consider Caruso a suspect.

And to top it all off, today was the day he got to try on his cowboy suit!

"Martino! My bath! This morning—lily of the valley."

Poor Luigi Davila, Caruso thought dutifully, not really meaning it. But

93

someone ought to mourn his passing. Caruso wondered if anyone in the world had loved the man, if there were anyone who would miss him. He thought it unlikely.

In his bath he started making the mental transition from *I Pagliacci* to *La Fanciulla del West*. He sang a little of the love duet from Act II to get himself in the mood, but his thoughts kept straying to his costume. A real six-shooter!

Mario came in carrying the morning newspapers, with their rave reviews of Caruso's *Pagliacci*. Caruso read them aloud as he ate his breakfast, translating into Italian those parts Martino and Mario could not follow. He was interrupted frequently by congratulatory telephone calls; even Puccini called. When he had finished reading the reviews, he went back and read them again. The tenor looked around. "Where's Ugo?"

"In his room," said Mario.

"Pouting," Martino added.

Caruso put down the papers. "*Now* what's the matter?"

The two valets just shook their heads; they hadn't asked.

Caruso decided he wouldn't ask either. Ugo got these moods sometimes.

Martino and Mario accompanied the tenor to the opera house, Martino to make any little adjustments Caruso's new costume might need and Mario to carry back the mail. As they waited on the corner of Thirty-ninth Street for the traffic light to change, Caruso looked across Broadway at the main entrance of the Metropolitan. The place didn't look like a yellow brick brewery to him; he wished people wouldn't call it that.

A horn sounded, and Caruso heard his name called out. A motor-car driver— whom he did not know— was leaning out the window and waving. Caruso smiled and waved back, and thoughtfully watched the black Hupmobile coupé whiz away. *About eleven hundred dollars,* Caruso thought. But he liked the limousines better— perhaps an Alco. "Mario," he said, "do you think you could learn to drive a motor car?"

"I am willing to try, signore," Mario answered mournfully.

The light changed. Inside the Met, they found two bags of mail waiting; Mario would have to make a second trip. Backstage Caruso was repeatedly greeted with shouted congratulations for last night's *Pagliacci.*

Then he spotted Pasquale Amato, already dressed in his all-black sheriff's costume, looking quite menacing and very Old West.

"Pasquale!" Caruso cried out. "You are the most convincing villain I have ever seen!"

Amato twirled his mustache and sneered and then confessed, "I am reluctant to admit how comfortable I am in this bad-man outfit. I wish my wife could see me." He drew Caruso aside. "What about you, Rico? Are you all right?"

"I have never felt better," the tenor exulted as they strolled toward the stairs to the dressing rooms. "Everything is working out exactly right, yes?"

"Yes, but at such a price! Poor little blackmailer. He must have been more dangerous than we thought for someone actually to *kill* him. And poor Rico! That must have been dreadful for you, finding him like that. I feel responsible, you know. You would never have gone to see him if I had not suggested it."

The vision of Luigi Davila lying on the floor with a knife in his side flashed through Caruso's mind; quickly he thrust the image aside. "It was mildly disturbing, of course," he told Amato in the most blasé manner he could summon. "But I do what has to be done. First I quietly notify the police. Then I help them with their inquiries."

"And then you come here and sing what everyone is saying is the best *Pagliacci* ever. *Cielo!* And I missed it."

They started up the stairs to the dressing rooms but got only a few steps when they caught sight of Toscanini at the top. The conductor was huddled over something concealed in his hand; his face was one big scowl.

"Maestro?" Amato said.

Toscanini's head jerked up; his eyes grew large enough for the whites to show all the way around the pupils. He thrust his hand into his pocket and hurried down the stairs, muttering something unintelligible as he pushed past the two singers.

"What *is* that thing he keeps hiding from everybody?" Amato complained. "That is the third or fourth time I have seen him do that!"

"I too have seen it before," Caruso nodded. "He acts as if he is ashamed."

"Or guilty. Could our Maestro be guilty of some indiscretion?"

Caruso shook his head. "Not a very big indiscretion if he can carry it around in his pocket."

Amato laughed. "You are right. Come, let us go see your cowboy suit."

Martino had gone up ahead to the wardrobe chamber on the fourth floor and now had the costume ready for Caruso. As soon as he'd changed, Caruso posed dramatically for the other two men—who laughed and applauded. The shirt and belt were both lightly fringed and worn under a suede jacket. The oversized cowboy hat sat lightly on the tops of the tenor's ears. Caruso's stomach bulged over the top of his tight-fitting pants, but never mind. The "boots" were made like spats, to be pulled on over regular shoes—but these went all the way up over the tenor's knees. He had a gun on one hip and a knife on the other. A bandanna tied around his neck gave him a rakish air.

But what delighted Caruso most of all was something he hadn't even thought of: spurs. Not little light jingly things, but big, *heavy, clanking spurs!* He did a few turns around the dressing room, clank clank clank.

"Rico, you are a Wild West bandit come

to life!" Martino marveled.

Amato agreed. "That is exactly what Puccini had in mind, I am sure! Shall we go? It is almost time to start."

Martino stayed behind while the two singers went down to the stage level, Caruso clanking all the way. Amato's valet came running up to him with a watch chain the baritone had forgotten. Caruso wandered away, looking at the other costumes. Emmy Destinn was having trouble adjusting her neck scarf; her maid Sigrid kept picking at her—adjusting a fold here, straightening a seam there, until Emmy snapped at her to stop. David Belasco was inspecting the chorus members, all of whom seemed to be having a good time in their strange outfits—strange for opera, that was.

"Ah, Enrico! You have recovered from yesterday's ordeal, I see!" Gatti-Casazza had come up behind him. "Let me look at you—why, I would have mistaken you for a real cowboy!"

"Very authentic, yes? And listen!" Caruso clanked a few steps away, then back.

"Oh dear, I don't know what Maestro Toscanini will think about that," the general manager worried. "But I must admit those spurs do add a certain something. Is the costume comfortable, Enrico?"

"Exceedingly comfortable. I am thinking of having one made up for my personal use."

"I hope Mr. Belasco is pleased." Gatti-Casazza glanced over to where the stage director was talking earnestly to Emmy Destinn.

"Madame Destinn," Belasco was saying patiently, "California mining camps were rough, primitive places. The women there did not wear silk stockings."

"*I* wear silk stockings," Emmy said stoutly.

"Of course you do. But a girl running a saloon for miners wouldn't. You are that girl, you are Minnie. And Minnie must wear cotton stockings."

Emmy screamed, a nice A-flat. "*Cotton* stockings! I *never* wear cotton stockings!"

"Nevertheless, that is what Minnie must wear," Belasco said calmly.

"I will wear silk stockings."

Caruso whispered, "Which one will win, do you think?"

Gatti-Casazza smiled. "Mr. Belasco has the gift of getting people to do things the way he wants them done."

That was true, Caruso thought. Belasco never raised his voice, never got excited; but people listened when he spoke. His ecclesiastical garb undoubtedly gave him authority with the religious Italians in the cast, but Emmy Destinn was neither Italian nor obtrusively religious. "I think I put my money on Emmy," Caruso said.

Belasco was coming toward them, reading a list he'd made out. "A most remarkable cast, Mr. Gatti," he said in his soft voice. "Ten Italians, one American, one Bohemian, one Pole, one Spaniard, one Frenchman, and two Germans. All dressed as cowboys and all singing Italian."

"A fine cast indeed," Gatti-Casazza beamed.

"We're having some difficulty in communicating, however," Belasco smiled. "But that's not what I wanted to speak to you about. It's the matter of costumes—your gold miners really should not be wearing cowboy suits, sir."

"But, but, but Puccini wrote explicitly in the score that they *were* to be dressed as cowboys!"

"Nevertheless, such dress is inaccurate.

I was born in California, and I traveled extensively through the mining country in my youth. And believe me, Mr. Gatti, gold miners do *not* wear riding chaps and ten-gallon hats."

"Oh dear, oh dear." The general manager plucked his beard. "I suppose I could speak to Puccini about it . . . ."

"Perhaps I should speak to him?"

"If you like," Gatti-Casazza said with obvious relief. "Not dressed as cowboys! Oh dear."

Caruso glared after the departing priestly figure. "He will not take away my six-shooter! I do not permit it!"

"Of course not, Enrico. It is only the miners he is concerned about."

Quickly mollified, Caruso stepped onto the stage and looked to the back of the auditorium. "By the way, where is Puccini?" he asked Gatti-Casazza. "I have not seen him today."

"Come to think of it, neither have I. Oh well, I suppose he's around somewhere."

The sound of a baton rapping sharply in the orchestra pit caught their attention; it was time to begin. "Madame Destinn! Mr. Amato! Mr. Caruso! Places, please."

The music stand in front of Toscanini was empty; from here on he would conduct without a score.

They were ready to rehearse the poker game. As a wounded fugitive, Caruso would hide in the loft of the girl's cabin while she tried to get rid of the sullen, brutal sheriff who was chasing him. But he would be betrayed by a drop of blood falling through the rafters onto the sheriff's hand. Then Caruso would have to drag his poor, wounded body down the ladder from the loft and collapse at a table while the girl and the sheriff played cards for his life. It was a good scene, full of musical tension and rising excitement. But it was the soprano's and the baritone's scene; all Caruso had to do was lie there and bleed. But he would bleed *beautifully.*

"All the way through!" Toscanini called. "No interruptions!"

The three singers on the stage looked at him skeptically but nodded agreement.

The scene commenced, and Toscanini kept his word— almost. He had to stop them once, at a point where the orchestra was playing in one tempo and the soloists singing in another. The conductor quickly got everybody back together, and the scene proceeded. During the part where the tenor slumped at the table while the girl of the Golden West cheated at cards to save her man, Caruso opened one eye and spotted a cigarette glowing at the back of the auditorium. Ah, Puccini was there.

Puccini was very much there— as everyone discovered as soon as the scene was finished. The composer rushed down the aisle, embraced Toscanini, and threw compliments to the orchestra. Next he was on the stage, embracing his soprano, his baritone, and his tenor. Then he was at the edge of the stage, paying more compliments to Toscanini.

"I think he liked it," Amato said wryly.

Caruso was astonished; he'd never seen the composer so demonstrative before. Puccini's eyes were glittering and he couldn't seem to stand still— he was all over the place. Such enthusiasm was contagious, and soon everyone was as keyed up as the man who'd written the opera.

It was the best rehearsal day they'd had yet.

But at last they had to stop; it was time for the stagehands to start putting up the set for that evening's performance of *Il Trovatore* (some other tenor that night, a fellow named Slezak). A pity—everyone wanted to keep going.

"Caruso, have dinner with me tonight," Puccini said exuberantly. "I insist!"

The tenor had been planning to attend a dinner party, but he accepted Puccini's invitation without hesitation. "As soon as I change my clothing," he said.

In his dressing room he told Martino he wanted him to deliver a note; he would write his apologies to the very nice society lady who was giving the dinner party. It was to be a large party; one tenor more or less wouldn't be missed. Caruso knew that wasn't strictly true, but he was too eager to talk to Puccini alone to let a little thing like a prior engagement get in the way.

But when he sat at the small writing table he kept in his dressing room and took out pen and paper, he found to his chagrin that he couldn't remember his hostess's name. His mind was blank. He'd sung at musicales at her Fifth Avenue mansion and he certainly should remember her *name. Cielo,* her family had helped *found* the Metropolitan Opera—her name, her name! "Martino, what is the name of the lady who gives the dinner party tonight? I cannot remember."

Martino frowned. "I do not think you told me, Rico."

"Of course I told you. A very big name in New York society. The lady who always hums off-key during performances."

Martino shook his head. "You told me you go to a dinner party tonight, but that is all."

"Eh, well, I do not go anyway." But he couldn't just fail to show up without the courtesy of an explanation. What to do?

Emmy! Emmy Destinn was going to the same party—she could tell him the name. Caruso scribbled a hasty note and told Martino to take it to Emmy's dressing room. By the time Martino got back, the tenor was out of his cowboy suit, which would have to be cleaned and pressed before he could wear it again.

He had just finished dressing when Emmy Destinn's maid pushed open the door and walked in without knocking. "Madame Destinn says she cannot read your handwriting," Sigrid announced, holding the note out scornfully at arm's length. "Look at that! Chicken scratches."

"Sigrid," Martino said reprovingly.

Caruso sighed; why did this woman go out of her way to aggravate him? "I merely want to ask her the name of our hostess tonight."

"You do not know the name of your hostess?"

"Of course I know her name. I just temporarily forgot it, that's all."

Sigrid's mouth dropped open. "You forgot the name of *Mrs. Cornelius Vanderbilt?!*"

"Vanderbilt!" Caruso cried, throwing up his arms. "Of course!"

"Ah, Mrs. Vanderbilt, yes," Martino smiled, and hustled Sigrid out of the dressing room. Caruso sat down and wrote a second note, this time being careful with his handwriting. A sudden indisposition, he claimed. Martino took the note to deliver and Caruso went downstairs to find Puccini.

Puccini asked Caruso to select the restaurant, and the tenor chose a little-known place called Sanella's on West Forty-seventh that he'd only recently discovered. He didn't want Mrs. Cornelius Vanderbilt reading in the paper tomorrow that the world's greatest composer and the world's greatest tenor had been seen dining out together the night before.

Feathery December snow was falling by the time they reached Sanella's. They were seated and served with a minimum of fuss. When they were alone Puccini said, "I have been dying to ask you all day, Caruso. What were you doing in Luigi Davila's office? Why did you go to see him?"

Caruso explained what he'd had in mind. "I thought, if he knows *I* know he is a blackmailer, he will not be so eager to go ahead with his little scheme, yes? But I never spoke to him about it. He had already been dead for a day by the time I got there."

"What did you tell the police?"

"Aha!" Caruso was rather pleased with this part. "I tell them I go see him on business, to arrange a few little singing engagements. Your name is never even mentioned, Puccini."

The composer looked dubious. "And they believe that? That you go there on business?"

Caruso wasn't so pleased with this part. "Not completely. But what can they do? I say I go on business, they cannot prove otherwise. All we have to do is keep quiet, say nothing. You are safe, my friend."

A tentative smile appeared on the composer's face. "I am safe, aren't I?" he said softly. "You don't know how that feels, Caruso, having that weight off my shoulders! I also feel guilty — finding my own release through the death of another man. I know I should be sorry he is dead. But I'm not, Caruso. God forgive me, I am not sorry. I am glad he's dead. I cannot help myself."

The tenor made properly sympathetic noises. "You are happy to be free, and you are ashamed of yourself for being happy. There is no need for shame. Think how much Davila must have been hated for someone to kill him! He was a bad man — you do not feel shame over one such as that."

"Hated or feared, one or the other," Puccini sighed. "Either way, I have been rescued from an appalling fate by someone whose name I do not even know."

"Do you want to know it?"

The composer shuddered. "No."

The talk turned to other things as they ate their rigatoni, laughing often and enjoying themselves. In spite of Caruso's assurances to Puccini, the tenor too was feeling slightly guilty that a man's death should be a cause of celebration. Luigi Davila got what he deserved; yet somehow it didn't seem right to say so. But it was over and done with now; no need to dwell on it.

The snow had stopped by the time they left the restaurant, and Puccini suggested they walk to his hotel. As they turned into Broadway, Caruso again felt the surge of pleasure New York at night always brought him. The light reflecting from the snow on the street made Broadway seem even brighter than usual. The most brilliantly lit thoroughfare in the world— no wonder they called it The Great White Way. It was said there were more globes burning in a ten-block stretch of Broadway than in the entire city of London, and Caruso believed it. New York was truly an electric city.

The illuminated billboard advertisements were everywhere. Mrs. Patrick Campbell in *The Foolish Virgin* at the Knickerbocker Theatre. Robert Burns Cigars and Dewar Scotch. William Gillette in *Sherlock Holmes* at the Empire, across Broadway from the Met. Studebaker, Spencerian Steel Pens, C and C Ginger Ale (Splits 15¢), Aunt Hannah's Death Drops. Sarah Bernhardt in repertoire at the Globe. Kremonia, Better Than Ammonia. Mlle. Dazie in *A Night in a Turkish Bath* at Hammerstein's Victoria.

Neither Caruso nor Puccini talked as they walked, both men enjoying the companionable silence. If there was one good thing to come out of this blackmailing business, Caruso thought, it was that he now felt closer to Puccini than ever before. The distance that had always separated them seemed to have disappeared.

The Hotel Buckingham was not much farther, fortunately, Fifth Avenue and Fiftieth; the cold was starting to make itself felt. Caruso was just beginning not to enjoy the walk when they reached the front entrance. Across the street, worshippers were hurrying into St. Patrick's Cathedral; or perhaps they were just people who wanted to get in out of the cold for a while. Puccini invited Caruso in for a little liquid warmth.

The Buckingham's overheated lobby was a shock to their systems. They were hastily shedding their overcoats when Caruso spotted a lanky, derby-wearing Irishman unwinding himself from the chair he'd been sitting in.

"Evening, Mr. Caruso," Lieutenant O'Halloran said pleasantly, and then turned to the other man. "Are you Giacomo Puccini?" He pronounced it *Jocky-mow*.

"I am," Puccini said. "Who are you, sir?"

"Lieutenant O'Halloran, Detective Bureau. I thought I'd just drop by and give you a chance to tell me why I shouldn't arrest you for murder."

SIX

LIEUTENANT O'HALLORAN HAD found the forged letters; it was as simple as that.

A routine police search of Luigi Davila's office after the murder had turned up a packet of four letters signed "Elvira Puccini." O'Halloran had had them translated into English and found their contents quite interesting. Mostly they were concerned with the kind of poison to be used. One letter expressed the wish that "the whore Doria" not die too quickly.

"Who's Doria?" the detective wanted to know.

In Puccini's hotel suite, the composer poured out the whole story of misunderstanding and jealousy that had led to the servant girl's tragic suicide. When he got to the part about bribing Doria's family to withdraw the charges against his wife, he hesitated.

"I think," Caruso said unhappily, "you had better tell him everything."

So Puccini explained how he'd been able to circumvent the court's decision by writing one very large check. When he finished, there was an ominous silence.

Lieutenant O'Halloran took off his derby, looked inside, put it back on. "Is that the way they do things in your country?"

"Yes," Puccini said without elaboration, mildly surprised at the question.

"It is a solution that satisfies everyone," Caruso offered helpfully. "Doria's family are poor people— is that not true, Puccini? Sending Elvira to prison does not help them. But the money— ah, the money is something they can use. And the court is satisfied because, ah, reconstitution is made to the family."

"Reconstitution? Oh— restitution."

"Yes, restitution. So you see, Lieutenant, it is the best solution for everybody."

"I wonder if Doria would agree," O'Halloran said dryly. But then he thought of New York's own coroner's court, as corrupt as they came, and decided he was in no position to criticize. "Mr. Puccini, you're saying the girl took her own life. But the letters show your wife was arranging to have her killed—"

"Elvira did not write those letters!" Puccini said hotly. "They are forgeries, Lieutenant! Elvira did not hire a poisoner—the idea is absurd. It's a plot this Davila thought up. Those letters are forged."

"Oh, you saw them, then?"

"I saw one of them. Davila said the others were just like it. I told him I knew Elvira had not written them—but he said would the police believe that?"

O'Halloran was thinking. "Do you have some samples of your wife's handwriting? Some letters she's written you? We have a man at the station house who's made a study of handwriting. He ought to be able to tell us whether Davila's letters are forgeries or not."

A look of hope flickered across Puccini's face. "Yes, of course. I'll get them." He got up and left the room. O'Halloran lounged after him, watching from the doorway.

"There is no back exit," Caruso said

crossly. "He is not going to run away." O'Halloran just smiled.

Puccini returned with two letters. "Here you are, Lieutenant. Can your man really prove Elvira did not write those others?"

"We'll see," O'Halloran said noncommittally. "Even if she didn't write them, Davila could still have made a lot of trouble for you, couldn't he, Mr. Puccini? What would the folks back home think if they knew about those letters? Do you think you could buy your way out of that one?"

Puccini raised one hand in the air. "Please. That is all I have been thinking of for the past week. If the Italian authorities believed those letters to be authentic, there is no way in the world I could save Elvira this time. And she is innocent! But I could not buy her freedom again."

"Which gives you a pretty good motive for murder," O'Halloran said pointedly.

Caruso was on his feet, shouting. *"Non è vero, sono discorsi in aria—"*

"English, Mr. Caruso, English."

"You talk nonsense! Puccini did not kill Davila— or anyone else! He is a creator, not a destroyer! You insult him—"

"Hold it, Mr. Caruso. Somebody 'insulted'

Luigi Davila pretty badly, and it's my job to find out who. Now it seems clear Davila was blackmailing Mr. Puccini here, but I'd say it hadn't been going on for very long. How much had you paid him so far, Mr. Puccini?"

"Nothing," the composer said. "We were, ah, negotiating — that is the correct term? He wanted me to support him. For the rest of his life. I had not started paying him yet."

"But you were going to?"

Puccini shrugged. "I suppose so. But I did not kill him. The thought never even occurred to me." His face was taking on a pinched look.

"Davila was killed the day before yesterday, on Monday," O'Halloran said, "about twenty-four hours before Mr. Caruso found him. Where were you Monday in the afternoon?"

"He was at the opera house," Caruso said before Puccini could speak.

O'Halloran cocked an eyebrow at him. "All afternoon?"

"All afternoon."

"How can you be so sure?"

"He is there every afternoon," Caruso stated flatly just as Puccini said, "I am there every afternoon."

"*Every* afternoon?"

"Ask anybody!" Caruso exclaimed. "We all see him, he comes to every rehearsal. Ask anybody."

"I intend to do just that." The detective paused. "Davila wasn't a very successful blackmailer, was he? The way he lived and all. A man who'd made money out of blackmail surely wouldn't have stayed in a place like that— don't you agree, Mr. Puccini?"

Puccini looked puzzled. "A place like what, Lieutenant? Do you mean his home or his place of business? I never saw either of them."

"They are the same," Caruso started to explain. "He lived in one room behind— "

"You never saw his place, Mr. Puccini?" O'Halloran cut in.

"No, I told you I did not." The composer narrowed his eyes. "That was a trap, yes? To see if I had been there?"

"*He* was not there," Caruso declared. "*I* was there."

"Oh yes, about that. Are you ready to tell me now why you were really there, Mr. Caruso? Why did you go to see Davila?"

The tenor cleared his throat and tried not to look foolish. "I think perhaps I can talk him out of it. The blackmail, I mean."

O'Halloran stared at him. "Talk him out of it? A blackmailer?" He pursed his lips and whistled tunelessly. "I think I liked your first story better."

Caruso shrugged. "Eh, well, I went to see him about a concert tour," he said agreeably.

"Don't play games with me!" O'Halloran barked, making the other two men jump. "Now tell me the truth, Mr. Caruso! Why were you there?"

Caruso gave a drawn-out sigh. "I think you do not believe me, whatever I say. But I did go to see if I can persuade him to abandon his plan to blackmail my friend. I think if he knows *I* know, he will be afraid to proceed."

"You went there to bully him into backing down."

Caruso's eyebrows shot up. "I? Bully? I never bully. I *persuade.*"

"Same difference," O'Halloran muttered. "So Puccini sends you to try your luck—"

"No, no! Puccini does not send me. I send myself. Puccini does not even know I am going."

"That is true," Puccini nodded.

O'Halloran stared at them both a long time, wondering how much of their story he should believe. He decided to put off deciding. "All right, Mr. Puccini, I'm not going to place you under arrest, at least not now." He paused for the double sigh of relief that greeted his announcement. "I want to check your alibi and get our handwriting expert to study these letters. But I don't want either of you to leave New York or even change your hotels— you're at the Knickerbocker, aren't you, Mr. Caruso? I want to be able to find you at any time of the day."

The two Italians hastily assured him that they were not going anywhere. Then Puccini said, "Lieutenant, may I ask you a question now? How many people know about those forged letters? Besides yourself."

"My superior. The officer who translated them. And the handwriting expert will know. Three people— four, counting me."

"You have not mentioned any of this to the newspapers?"

"Not yet. Why? What would you do if we did?"

Puccini looked away. "Rather than go through another scandal? I think I would kill myself!"

O'Halloran gave a snort of derisory laughter. Italians! So theatrical—always talking about grand passions and suffering and the like. "Scandal isn't fatal," he said shortly. "People don't kill themselves over scandal any more."

"Doria," Caruso said simply.

The police detective had the grace to look embarrassed. "You're right, I forgot about her. But she was a young girl—she couldn't have had much experience of the world. Look, Mr. Puccini, I'm not trying to make trouble for you. If you are innocent of murder and your wife did not write those letters, I give you my promise not one word of this will ever reach the press. But if either of you is guilty—then I also give you my promise that *everybody* is going to know about it. Including the authorities in Italy. Understand?"

"All too well, Lieutenant," Puccini said. "It never stops."

O'Halloran warned them again about changing their addresses and offered Caruso a ride back to the Knickerbocker. The tenor extracted a promise from Puccini that he wouldn't do anything foolish and accepted the detective's offer.

As the two men stood in the lobby putting on their coats, Caruso said, "Lieutenant O'Halloran, there is something I do not wish to ask you in front of Puccini. So I ask you now. This Luigi Davila, he is Black Hand, yes? No?"

O'Halloran grinned. "I was wondering when you'd get around to that. No, he wasn't, as a matter of fact. As far as we can find out, he never had anything to do with those terrorists— that was one of the first things we looked into. It's not the Black Hand this time. Davila was acting alone."

Caruso smiled, the first time in an hour. "That is good news. Puccini has been through so much lately— to think the Black Hand is after him too . . ." He trailed off.

O'Halloran started to open the lobby door but paused. "Mr. Caruso, you seem like a decent fellow. Let me caution you about putting too much faith in your friend Puccini. He could be a killer, you know."

Caruso bristled. "Puccini would never kill anyone! It is a preposterous idea."

"There, that's what I'm talking about.

He's your friend, and so you can't even imagine him as a murderer. But you saw how Davila was living—did that look like the place of a man who'd been in the blackmail business for long? It's beginning to look as if your friend Puccini was his only victim."

Caruso sputtered, "There can be other reasons for killing besides blackmail!"

"And we're looking for them," the detective assured him. "But so far it seems the only one with a motive for killing Davila is Jocky-mow Puccini."

"Giacomo," Caruso corrected him testily. "You are wrong, Lieutenant O'Halloran. Wrong, wrong, wrong, wrong, *wrong!*"

"Maybe. Just be careful."

Caruso snarled a fine Neapolitan curse and pushed through the lobby door into the winter night. How could a world that looked so bright in the morning turn to ashes before midnight? In less than twenty-four hours, everything had been turned inside out. Puccini was not free, he was not safe; now he had a bigger threat hanging over him than ever.

Giacomo Puccini, a murderer! Caruso shook his head in disbelief. How could

Lieutenant O'Halloran be so obtuse? No sane man would ever seriously suspect Puccini of being a killer. Even now Caruso had trouble believing O'Halloran's suspicions were anything more than a cruel joke.

It had been a long day. When the detective let him out of the police motor car at the Hotel Knickerbocker in Times Square, Caruso was seized with an urgent need to talk to somebody. It was too late to go bursting in on Pasquale Amato, and the only other person who knew about Davila's attempt to blackmail Puccini was Ugo. But Ugo's door was locked; he was still pouting.

Caruso had trouble falling asleep that night.

The next morning he had to put Puccini's troubles aside long enough to deal with a small domestic crisis. He was only half dressed when it came out why Ugo had spent the previous day pouting.

Mario's new suit.

"I *tell* him to buy a new suit, Ugo," Caruso said. "I do not want my valets looking shabby."

"Then let him look not shabby for less

money!" Ugo protested. "Do you know how much he spends for the suit? Eighteen dollars! *Eighteen dollars,* Rico. That is three dollars more than a member of the Metropolitan Opera chorus earns in a week!"

Mario looked mournful and said nothing.

Martino tried to help. "Eighteen dollars is not so much money for a good suit, Ugo. And prices do keep going up."

"He is taking advantage of you, Rico," Ugo said, ignoring Martino. "Eighteen dollars for a suit!"

Caruso looked his disgruntled valet straight in the eye. "Do you want a new suit, Ugo?"

"No, I do not want a new suit! I want you to stop wasting money! Tell him to take it back, Rico. Take it back and exchange it for something cheaper."

"Eh, well," Caruso said. "Clearly there is only one thing to be done. Mario!"

The young valet lifted his sad eyes.

"You are to return the new suit. Take it back and exchange it for a *forty*-dollar suit!"

"Forty dollars!" Ugo screeched. Mario looked stunned, while Martino just laughed. "Rico, you don't mean that!" Ugo cried.

"Ah, but I do! A forty-dollar suit, Mario,

do you hear? Not a penny less. And Ugo, not one more word about this matter! No complaining, no pouting in your room— *not a word!*" he said sharply, as Ugo started to speak. "I have more important matters on my mind. You must not bother me with trifles at a time like this."

"What is it, Rico?" Martino asked, concerned. "What is the matter?"

Caruso looked at the three of them and wondered if Ugo had kept his word about not telling the other two of the blackmail. This might be a good time to find out. "The police," he said slowly, "suspect Puccini of murdering Luigi Davila."

Martino's cry of distress could have been a woman's scream. "No, it is impossible! Mr. Puccini a murderer? How can they even think such a thing! And Luigi Davila? Why, Mr. Puccini would have nothing to do with a man like that! Are you sure, Rico?"

Ugo pressed his lips together, not speaking; Mario looked confused. "I am sure," Caruso said. "Last night Lieutenant O'Halloran practically accused him to his face. And then later he warned me to be careful. He thinks Puccini killed Luigi Davila, no question of it."

"He is crazy!" Martino said emphatically. "Anyone who knows Mr. Puccini would never think a thing like that!"

"Who is Luigi Davila?" Mario asked.

"Bah! Such an innocent!" Ugo spat out. "Luigi Davila is the dead man Rico found, dummy!"

Mario's mouth formed an O and his eyes grew wide. "And the police think Mr. Puccini killed him?"

"But why?" Martino asked. "*Why* do they think so? Did Mr. Puccini know him? Luigi Davila was a dreadful man," he said to Mario. "He once tried to bribe me! To get to Rico."

Caruso was convinced that neither Martino nor Mario knew about the blackmail. Ugo, he noticed, had not offered an opinion. He started to ask him but then hesitated. He thought a moment. "Martino, I want you to go to Puccini and see if he is all right. Invite him to have breakfast with me. He will probably refuse, but invite him just the same."

"Yes, certainly. Perhaps there is something I can do for him." He hurried away.

That took care of Martino. "Mario,"

Caruso said, "I want you to mix up a new solution of throat spray. Put more salt water in it this time. And do it now, please—I want to take it with me to rehearsal."

"Yes, signore, right away." Mario left.

Caruso looked at his remaining valet. "Well, Ugo? What are you thinking?"

Ugo's eyes glittered. "I know Mr. Puccini is your friend, Rico—but he could have done it, yes? He could have killed the blackmailer."

Caruso was shocked. "Ugo! How can you say such a thing! Puccini is no killer."

"He had good reason, Rico."

"Yes, yes, that is what Lieutenant O'Halloran keeps saying. But no matter how good the reason, Puccini could never kill anyone. Not even a blackmailer."

They were interrupted by a sharp *rat-a-tat-tat* at the door—which Ugo opened to reveal a smiling Pasquale Amato standing there, his face still ruddy from the winter cold.

"Good morning, Rico! It is a clear December day, the snow is crisp and clean upon the ground, and I have come to take you to breakfast! So finish dressing, my friend, and we will go out into this beautiful day and . . . *what on earth is the matter?"* He'd finally noticed the expressions on their faces.

"The police think Puccini killed Davila," Caruso said bluntly. "Help me finish dressing, Ugo."

Tenor and valet went into the former's bedroom, leaving Amato standing by the door with his mouth open.

For the first time in more years than he could remember, Caruso didn't finish his meal.

"You must really be upset," Amato said, eyeing the cream pastry with one bite taken out of it. They hadn't gone out after all, eating instead in the Knickerbocker dining room, where Puccini could find them if he decided to accept Caruso's invitation to breakfast. "What did this Lieutenant O'Halloran say, exactly?"

"He said Puccini is the only one they find who has a motive." The tenor told his friend in detail what had happened the night before. "Just being accused can make a man look so guilty! Ugo has already started to wonder whether Puccini might not be a murderer."

"Ugo? What does Ugo have to do with it?"

Caruso stirred the coffee he wasn't drinking. "Oh, he is there in the room when Puccini tells me about Davila—about the blackmail. He knows the whole story."

"Mm," Amato mused. "Do you think that is wise? Allowing him to stay and hear everything, I mean?"

"I do not know what Puccini is going to say before he says it, do I?" Caruso snarled—and was immediately contrite. "Ah—I am sorry, Pasquale. I am not myself this morning. The day starts off badly. Ugo complains about Mario's new suit and I am worried about Puccini—you understand."

"Don't concern yourself, Rico, I do understand. What did you say Ugo was complaining about?"

"A suit Mario bought. Ugo thinks he paid too much for it, and he didn't. Fuss, fuss, fuss. Oh, how Ugo likes to fuss!"

The baritone nodded. "He does complain a lot, doesn't he? A natural-born grumbler."

"Why does he do it?" Caruso asked, welcoming the change of subject. "Martino and Mario—they never complain. Only Ugo."

"I have a theory about that," Amato announced playfully. "Ugo's problem is that he is not sure how he fits into your family."

"My family?" Caruso was puzzled. "All my relatives are back in Naples."

"I mean your traveling family, the one that goes with you wherever you go. Consider. You are the papa, the provider, the head of the family. Martino is the mama, making sure the household runs smoothly. Barthélemy is the eldest son, helping Papa in the family business. Mario is the well-loved baby. And Ugo— Ugo is the child in the middle, the one whose role is not clear."

Caruso looked at his friend askance. "Pasquale, that is the silliest thing I have ever heard you say!"

Amato laughed. "Why do you have three valets anyway, Rico? I get along perfectly well with only one."

"Too much work for one person. I need them all."

"Do you? Emmy Destinn needs only one maid, and she has almost as many clothes as you do. And Puccini is making do with no valet at all, now that his new man has run out on him."

They were back to Puccini. "He is not coming, is he?" Caruso said, looking at his pocket watch. "I worry about him, Pasquale. Last night he said something about killing himself if those forged letters are made public."

"Ah, well, he is under stress. People make extreme statements when they are under stress."

"But he has thought of suicide before! Right after Doria died—when it looked as if Elvira would go to prison. He blames himself for what happened." Caruso shook his head in wonder. "He blames himself!"

Amato nodded, seeing the composer's point of view. "Puccini is one of those people who turn their anger inward, who punish themselves instead of hitting out at others. If he were going to kill anyone, he should have thought of killing Elvira for making so much trouble. But he still loves her in spite of everything—he does, you know. And his own hands are not completely clean. So whom does he punish? Himself."

"I do not understand that at all," Caruso muttered. "People hurt you, you hurt them back. You do not hurt yourself *more*."

His friend smiled. "Puccini is a very complicated man—he does not have the direct response to life that you do, Rico. In a way, you are better equipped to survive than he is. Puccini would be more likely to kill himself than an enemy like Luigi Davila."

"So how can Lieutenant O'Halloran think he is guilty?" Caruso proclaimed loudly, attracting the attention of three or four other diners.

Amato turned his palms up. "Your Lieutenant O'Halloran does not know Puccini the way we do. And even if he did, it would probably make no difference. Policemen do not think the way other people do," he finished trenchantly. "All they care about are clues and evidence and matters of that sort."

Caruso snorted. "So what do we do? What do I do? How do I help Puccini?"

"Do?" Amato shrugged. "What is there to do? I see nothing you can do—unless you find the real killer yourself."

Caruso let a smile spread slowly across his face. "Ah. Aha."

"Rico?" Amato said, alarmed that the tenor had taken him seriously. "You are not thinking—"

"Yes," Caruso nodded, his smile now full-blown. "That is what I do. I find the real killer myself."

"Rico, don't be crazy! You cannot solve a crime the police themselves are having trouble with!"

"How do you know I cannot solve a crime? I have never tried before."

"And you are not going to try now! Be sensible. You are a *singer*, not a detective!"

"Perhaps I am detective too. I have more than one string to my bow! I am a versatile man," he proclaimed proudly, liking this image of himself. "I can improvise when I need to. It is like singing a cadenza, Pasquale. You take charge of the music yourself."

Amato threw up his hands, got up from the table in annoyance, and left the tenor to pay the bill. Caruso carefully wrote the amount down in his notebook.

SEVEN

"HE WANTS TO do *what?!*" Emmy Destinn was astounded.

"He wants to give us kissing lessons," Caruso said apologetically. "Mr. Belasco says we are not doing it right." What he'd actually said was that *Caruso* wasn't doing it right — but no need to tell Emmy that. "Let us indulge him, Emmy," Caruso grinned. "It might be fun!"

Emmy rolled her eyes and walked away.

Caruso was in a more cheerful frame of mind than he'd been in earlier in the morning. When he and Amato arrived at the Metropolitan, they'd found Puccini already there, a new look of determination on his face. "I will see this through," he'd told the tenor. "I survived before, I can survive again. I will fight this ignominious accusation!"

"And I will help you!" Caruso answered enthusiastically. He was delighted with the composer's new attitude — that, coupled with his own resolution to *do something*, had got his juices flowing again. There was only one small problem.

How did one go about solving a murder?

Maestro Toscanini wanted to start out with the third and final act of *Fanciulla*, the one in which the chorus figured so prominently. It was the point in the story where the miners turned into an ugly lynch mob, and Caruso was the man they wanted to hang. David Belasco was on the stage, trying to convince the unwieldy chorus to show more restraint.

"You must learn the value of *repose* on stage," he was saying. "No more un-motivated actions, please — no shrugging your shoulders, no grimacing, no gesticulating with your hands. Do you understand?"

The fifty chorus members responded by nodding vigorously, shrugging their shoulders, and gesticulating with their hands.

Belasco tried again. "The men who settled

the Old West were an uncommunicative lot. They did not give away their feelings through gestures and facial expressions. Some of you tend to make faces, and all of you wave your arms too much—whenever you feel like it, it seems, regardless of what's happening in the story. You must be more reserved, like the Westerners you portray."

"*Simple* men," Toscanini said helpfully, "for whom Puccini has written the appropriate music. You sing in unison or in octaves—no sophisticated harmonies for you! Be *simple*. Listen to Mr. Belasco, do as he says."

"*Ben volentieri!*" "Sure thing, Maestro." The men of the chorus started moseying off the stage at Belasco's gesture of dismissal.

Caruso went up to the stage director. "I do not think Emmy is too happy about practicing the kiss."

Belasco was unperturbed. "I'll speak to her later." He watched the last of the chorus trail off into the wings. The first time Belasco had seen the chorus make its entrance, he'd been appalled. Tenors and baritones and basses had trooped out onto the stage by the score, lined up in rows, and turned themselves into an arm-waving backdrop for the soloists. "If they would only stop *wriggling,*" Belasco lamented. "There's something you and Mr. Amato need to rehearse," he said to Caruso, "but it will have to wait — I think Maestro Toscanini is ready to begin."

The rehearsal started, and Caruso was surprised to see Puccini watching from the wings instead of his usual place at the back of the auditorium. The chorus members proceeded to work themselves up into a lynch mob ready to slip a rope over the tenor's head. Then it was time for *Ch'ella mi creda* — the first aria Caruso had ever sung that ended with his neck in a noose.

The aria was short and relatively simple, but Caruso loved it so much he gave it all he had. When he'd finished, the chorus burst into thunderous applause punctuated by cries of "Bravo!" — even though there was no break in the music at that point. Caruso fully expected a roar of outrage from the orchestra pit, but even Toscanini was clapping his hands.

In the wings, Puccini nodded approval. Caruso wanted to gesture modestly but his hands were tied behind his back. "Such a beautiful aria!" he called to Puccini. "Singing it is like a caress to the throat. Exquisite!"

"Ah yes," the composer said dismissively. "But it's so *Puccini!*"

"Now that we've stopped," Belasco said, walking back out on the stage. Toscanini was delivering an impassioned lecture to the orchestra's horn section, so Belasco used the time to work out a little stage business. At the end of the aria, Pasquale Amato was supposed to slap Caruso; the other times they'd rehearsed it, the slap had looked phony—because the baritone had pulled his punch, not wanting to hurt his friend. Belasco showed Amato how to swing his extended arm so the tips of his fingers missed Caruso's nose by a bare inch or so. Then he showed Caruso how to jerk his head to the side at just the right moment so it would look as if he'd been hit hard.

"But there is no sound that way," Amato objected. "The audience will know it is fake if there is no sound."

Caruso pretended to be hurt. "Do you really want to slap me, Pasquale?"

"There will be sound," Belasco assured them. He positioned one of the chorus members out of sight in back of Caruso and told him to clap on cue, showing him how to cup his hands to produce a louder sound. The three of them practiced the slap until Belasco was satisfied.

"We continue!" Toscanini cried.

Emmy Destinn marched out onto the stage. "When do I get my horse?" she demanded.

"Final dress rehearsal," Belasco told her.

"That is not enough time."

"Madame Destinn, you ride in and dismount immediately. One rehearsal with the horse will be enough."

"I do not like horses. I will need more time."

"*If* you please!" Toscanini bellowed. "We worry about your horse later, yes? Right now we *sing.*"

The soprano stalked off. The music started. Emmy walked on majestically, not deigning to pantomime riding and dismounting. The opera called for her literally to come riding to the rescue. She'd talk the miners out of lynching Caruso (she'd *sing* them out of it, rather); and *La Fanciulla del West* would end with the girl and her bandit lover going off arm-in-arm into the sunset.

A happy ending – unusual for a Puccini opera.

Belasco had divided the large chorus into smaller groups and gave each group different stage movements. Unfortunately, the chorus members not only had difficulty remembering where they were supposed to move on what cue, they also kept forgetting which group they were in. Every time they made a mistake, they waved their arms to make up for it.

When the act was ended, Belasco separated the dozen worst offenders from the rest of the chorus and gave them special instructions. "Put your hands in your pockets and keep them there," he told them. "The whole time. The audience is never to see your hands. Can you do that?"

"It will be hard," one of them said earnestly.

"I know," Belasco sighed. "But try."

Toscanini announced a lunch break.

"Do not lose heart," Caruso said to Belasco. "They will learn to be still."

"They were still while you were singing *Ch'ella mi creda,*" Belasco remarked. "I don't suppose you know anything about mass hypnosis, do you?"

A man Caruso didn't know was talking to Pasquale Amato. The tenor heard Amato say, "Yes, he was here the entire afternoon."

The man said something Caruso couldn't make out.

"Well, of course not *all* the time," Amato replied shortly. "I was rehearsing, I had other things to attend to. But he was there, in the back of the auditorium."

The unknown man was from the police, then— checking on Puccini's alibi. Suddenly there seemed to be several unknown men walking around the stage and the backstage area. They were talking to the chorus members, Emmy Destinn, the other soloists, even Emmy's maid, Sigrid.

Caruso planted himself downstage center. "Lieutenant O'Halloran!" he sang out. "Where *are* you?"

"Back here, Mr. Caruso," came the now familiar Irish voice from the back of the auditorium.

Caruso peered into the darkness at the back and could see nothing. Then O'Halloran stepped out into the light and started down the aisle; Caruso left the stage and hurried to meet him. "Well, Lieutenant, are you convinced Puccini is here all of

Monday afternoon?"

"I'm convinced he could have slipped out at any time without anybody noticing," O'Halloran growled. "Look at this place! It's black as pitch back there under the overhang—even an owl couldn't see him from the stage."

"But every time the lobby door opens there is light. And his cigarette—yes, his cigarette! That is how I know when he is here—I can see the cigarette glowing in the dark!"

"That's how you know *when* he is here?"

"*That* he is here, *when* he is here—English is such an unbending language! You know what I mean."

O'Halloran shook his head. "Won't do, Mr. Caruso. Your friend could have been here Monday the whole time. Or he could have been gone an hour without being missed. That's all it would take to get to Davila's rooms on Irving Place, kill him, and get back here. One hour."

Caruso had a sinking feeling in the pit of his stomach. He'd once seen the outside of the prison they called the Tombs; it made him sick to think of Puccini shut up in that cold and forbidding place. "But he was here," he said despairingly.

"He does not want to believe that, Caruso." Puccini was coming up the aisle toward them. "He has made up his mind that I killed that man, and nothing is going to budge him. Isn't that right, Lieutenant?"

"Now, I didn't say I'd made up my mind, Mr. Puccini. My men are still questioning the people here. But so far we haven't found anyone who was watching you the whole time. But we're still investigating. The knife Davila was killed with was his own, by the way. He was using it to peel an apple— we found it on the floor."

"The letters," Puccini said tightly. "What does your handwriting expert say about the letters?"

"Inconclusive. Our man compared the letters written by your wife to the ones we found in Davila's office— and he says he doesn't *think* they were written by the same person. But he's not willing to swear to it in court. Says there are too many questionable passages. But even if he did testify that those letters are forgeries, *you* still wouldn't be in the clear, Mr. Puccini. Your wife could still be hurt by new suspicions— and so could you. Those letters spell trouble, authentic or not."

Puccini asked quietly, "Are you going to arrest me?"

O'Halloran shrugged. "That depends on the district attorney. If he decides we have a case, he's going to present all the evidence he has at the inquest and ask for a verdict of willful murder. And I mean *all* the evidence, Mr. Puccini."

"The letters. They'll be made public."

"Afraid so. I can keep 'em quiet until then, but no longer than that."

"I see." Puccini was thoughtful. "When is this inquest, Lieutenant?"

"December twelfth. You'll be notified of the time and place."

"December twelfth," Caruso repeated. "Two days after the *Fanciulla* première."

"Well, that's something, isn't it?" O'Halloran said with false heartiness. "You'll get to see your new opera once."

"*Once!*" Caruso and Puccini both threw up their hands.

Just then one of O'Halloran's men started up the aisle and the Lieutenant turned away to meet him. Caruso groped for some quick consolation to offer Puccini. "A nice lunch?"

"Oh, Mr. Puccini," O'Halloran called.

"You'll keep yourself available for the next hour or so, won't you?"

"If I must." To Caruso: "I'd better stay. Go, enjoy your lunch. I do not feel like eating anyway."

Caruso murmured a few comforting phrases and left to hunt up Pasquale Amato. He found him by the door of the greenroom, peeking inside. When Amato saw Caruso coming, he placed one finger over his lips, signaling silence. "He's doing it again," the baritone whispered.

Cautiously Caruso peered into the greenroom. There was Toscanini, huddled over something in his hand, a frown of intense concentration on his face. He moved his hand and his head, looking at whatever he held from different angles.

Then he became aware he was being watched, and both the hand and what it was holding disappeared into a pocket. "You spy on me!" the Maestro shouted. "All the time, you two spy on me!" He pushed past them, muttering under his breath.

The two singers lounged in the doorway, watching the conductor scuttle away. "Dirty pictures?" Amato suggested.

But Caruso couldn't get interested in this

146

lesser mystery. "Come, we go eat lunch," he said to Amato. "I must tell you what is happening. Things do not look good for Puccini."

They went to Pane's Restaurant, and over a dish of linguini the tenor told his friend about the upcoming inquest. "I do not understand Lieutenant O'Halloran," he admitted. "Sometimes he seems sympathetic to Puccini—but he goes right on trying to prove he is a murderer!"

"He probably has no choice," Amato said. "We know Puccini did not kill that impresario because we know what kind of man he is. But the police do not know. All they see is a man with a strong reason for wanting Davila dead."

"Pah!" Caruso said in disgust. "There must be hundreds of people who wanted Luigi Davila dead. Weaselly men like that have no friends. The police just do not know who those other people are."

"That is a possibility, of course. Some other blackmail victim, perhaps? Someone who had been paying for years and years and finally had enough?"

Caruso remembered the bareness of Davila's home/office and shook his head.

"Alas, no. He was living too poorly. No man with money lives like that."

"Well, then." Amato thought a moment. "Davila had been trying to eke out a living from the music business for a long time— did you not say he had been after you for years?"

"Ever since the first time I come to America."

"All right, say he finally reaches a low point in his life where he knows he will never get anywhere if he keeps on the same way he has been going. Say he is desperate. What does he do? He has gotten nowhere in the music world— so perhaps he should try something else."

"Blackmail."

"He looks around. He needs someone both well-to-do and susceptible to blackmail. Whom does he see? Puccini, of course— still vulnerable after the scandal of the servant girl's death. But does he stop there? Might he not find someone else equally vulnerable? Or even a dozen others? Perhaps the reason Luigi Davila was living so poorly is that he was just *getting started* on his new 'career.' "

Caruso paused with his fork halfway to his

mouth. "Just getting started?" He put the fork down. "Pasquale," he said slowly, "I think that's it! That must be. He was just getting started— yes! Pasquale, do you know what that means? We could be *surrounded* by people Davila tried to blackmail!"

Amato laughed. "I doubt that he was that ambitious. But if he approached even one more person other than Puccini— such an indiscretion could well have led to his premature demise."

"Lieutenant O'Halloran says the knife that killed Davila belonged to him. Perhaps the murder was not planned."

"Perhaps not. One thing still puzzles me— how did Davila know what Elvira Puccini's handwriting looked like? He had to have a sample in order to copy it. Where did he get it?"

"That is easy," Caruso said smugly, happy to be able to contribute. "He got it from Puccini's new valet— the one who ran away? Davila paid him to steal one of Elvira's letters."

Amato looked at him skeptically. "How do you know that?"

"I do not exactly *know* it," Caruso admitted, "but I am sure that is what happened. He tried to bribe Martino once, you know. Some trifling sum. Davila would go to Puccini's valet, that is what he would do. Besides, how else could he get a letter Elvira had written?"

"It does make sense," the baritone conceded. "That valet obviously felt no loyalty to Puccini. It could be just as you say."

At that moment they were interrupted by two women who came up to their table and asked for autographs. The women were young and pretty and full of life, and greatly impressed at finding two opera stars having lunch in the same restaurant where they ate. When Caruso and Amato had signed their menus, they chatted on, showing a willingness to linger. Amato looked a question at Caruso; Caruso shook his head *no*. The young women were disappointed at not being invited to sit down, but they said goodbye graciously and left.

Amato watched them go with obvious regret. "Rico, that is the first time I have ever known you to say no to a pretty woman."

Caruso started; a first in his life, and he had almost let it pass unnoticed! He felt his forehead. "Perhaps I am ill?"

"Perhaps you are more involved in Puccini's troubles than is good for you," Amato said pointedly. "Rico, there is nothing you can do. Stand by Puccini in his time of need, certainly— we will all do that. But accept the fact that there is nothing you can do to change his fate."

"You think he is doomed."

"I think that what's going to happen is going to happen, regardless of how much speculating you and I do over a plate of linguini. Come, now— stop brooding over the composer and start thinking of the composition. Think only of *Fanciulla.* The opera should occupy all our thoughts from now on."

Caruso knew his friend was right, but it was difficult to concentrate on proper breathing and correct phrasing and good tonal quality when there was a murderer on the loose. Luigi Davila had spent his life trying to make some kind of living out of the music business. Therefore if he had had another blackmail victim in addition to Puccini, that victim was more than likely connected to music in some way.

And that meant the killer was someone they all knew.

Gatti-Casazza had spent the morning away from his general manager's office, so it was a shock for him to come in and find the Metropolitan Opera House had been invaded by the police. They had questioned him as to Puccini's whereabouts on Monday afternoon; without missing a beat Mr. Gatti lied glibly and said he himself had spent every minute of the day at Puccini's side. The police detective had smiled sardonically and advised him to think twice before telling that story in court.

But eventually the intruders left, with one exception— a man Lieutenant O'Halloran left behind to keep an eye on Puccini. The opera house settled back into its routine. Toscanini had dismissed the chorus for the day; he wanted to spend the rest of the afternoon concentrating on the soloists' parts in Act I.

Right away they were in trouble. The curtain opened on a darkened stage, with only the glow of a cigar visible. Gradually the light came up to reveal the interior of a saloon. It was Pasquale Amato who was smoking the cigar; he dropped it and burned a hole in his pants.

Then two of the secondary soloists got into a shouting match for no discernible reason. In the orchestra pit Toscanini turned his back to the stage, folded his arms, and stood in icy silence while Gatti-Casazza settled the dispute.

Emmy Destinn complained that her high C came too early in the act, that she did not have sufficient warm-up time. Puccini replied she had plenty of time to warm up and refused to change it.

The opera called for one of the men in the saloon to be caught cheating at cards; Amato pinned a card to the man's chest to brand him a cheat. Unfortunately, the baritone was a mite careless in the way he wielded the pin and another shouting match broke out. Toscanini seethed while David Belasco handled that one.

Next in the story came a tussle between Amato and one of the other men, who pulls a gun on him. Emmy was to dash in and break up the fight by snatching away the gun. Belasco had rehearsed the three singers carefully, but something went wrong and Emmy took a left to the jaw.

Intermission.

"I can sing no more!" Emmy wailed. "I need a doctor! Will no one take me to a hospital?" Everyone crowded around her, sincerely commiserating but not really knowing what to do.

"Emmy, I am so sorry!" Amato groaned. "I don't know what happened—I do not mean to hit you! I am disconsolate! Forgive me, Emmy—say you forgive me?"

"I do *not* forgive you! I will never sing again. Oh!" She clutched her jaw in what might really have been pain.

Caruso had rushed in from the wings where he'd been watching. "It is an accident, Emmy—he does not want to hurt you—you know that. Look at him. He is inconsolable! Poor Pasquale would never deliberately hurt you."

"Will you please stop worrying about poor Pasquale and start thinking about poor Emmy? *I* am the one who got hit! Oh!"

Then Sigrid was there, elbowing her way none too gently through the crowd. She was carrying ice wrapped in a linen towel, which she held to Emmy's jaw. ("Where did she get ice so fast?" Amato asked Caruso.) Sigrid was making soothing noises, murmuring encouraging phrases in Swedish, which

154

Emmy didn't understand.

"Better?" Amato asked hopefully after a minute.

"Keep away!" Sigrid snarled, shaking a fist at him.

Gatti-Casazza, Toscanini, and Belasco conferred. "Shall I send for a doctor, Emmy?" the general manager asked.

"It does not matter," she answered grandly. "I can sing no more today."

"I am clumsy," Amato moaned. "I am an oaf. I do not deserve to be on the same stage with the great Emmy Destinn."

"How true," Emmy sighed.

"Hit me!" Amato demanded dramatically. "Hit me back, Emmy! It will make you feel better, and it is no more than I deserve." He held his arms stiffly at his sides and bravely thrust out his chin.

Emmy got a gleam in her eye.

A moment later, she made an announcement. "I am ready to resume," she told Toscanini, who was staring horrified at the flattened baritone.

Eventually they got Amato back on his feet, and no one suggested they rehearse the fight again. Toscanini started where they'd left off, and the rehearsal proceeded smoothly enough except for a slight tendency on Amato's part to wander around the stage with a dazed look on his face. Then they came to a part of the act where Emmy was supposed to read from the Bible.

Someone had glued the pages together.

As one person, cast, conductor, orchestra, composer, and general manager turned to look toward where their lead tenor was waiting in the wings. "CARUSO" they roared *ensemble*.

"What? What?" he cried, alarmed. "I do nothing!"

"You are *always* playing practical jokes," Puccini said angrily. "A world première we are preparing, and still you play jokes!"

"But I do nothing! You—"

"What about the time you brought a chamber pot onstage during *La Bohème?*" Emmy demanded.

"Or the times you sewed up the sleeves of my costumes?" Amato muttered.

"Pranks, pranks, pranks!" Toscanini shouted. "Like a little boy, always playing pranks!"

"Really, Enrico," Gatti-Casazza said reprovingly. "At a time like this? You should know better."

"But I do not do it! Someone else!"

Belasco took out a handkerchief and dabbed at his forehead. The police detective assigned to watch Puccini had the expression of a man who's just realized he's been trapped inside a lunatic asylum.

Caruso's feelings were hurt. They should know him better than to think he'd deliberately cause trouble for Puccini's new opera. Certainly, he had played little tricks in the past — but not now, not during *Fanciulla* rehearsal. He'd promised there'd be no practical jokes — and Mr. Gatti should know he did not break his promises! Over and over he told them he did not glue the Bible pages together, but no one listened! How terrible it was, being accused of something one had not done!

They started again. Amato was to declare his love to Emmy, only to be rejected. The passage contained some tricky parts for the baritone; Amato managed them all right but sang his passion to an empty chair while Emmy stood behind him with her fists on her hips. Then Caruso made his entrance. Belasco had directed him to sing his opening phrases with his back to the audience; when he turned around, everyone saw he was carrying a bottle and atomizer in one hand. Caruso sprayed his throat every time one of the others was singing.

Toscanini put down his baton. *"Mister* Caruso! Do you plan on carrying a spray bottle with you during the performance?"

"A soreness in the throat," Caruso said with a catch in his voice, hoping for a little sympathy from these hostile people. "It will not go away!"

"Too many cigarettes," Gatti-Casazza growled. Belasco quietly stepped out onto the stage and took the tenor's throat spray away from him.

Toscanini's face was red and the veins in his temple were pulsing, but he managed to contain himself. Once again they resumed. Caruso ordered a drink at the bar, which the bartender served him. Then Amato joined Caruso and Emmy there and, in a gesture meant as a challenge, knocked the tenor's glass off the bar. Alas, his aim was a little off and the colored water splashed all over Emmy's dress.

Emmy leaned one elbow heavily on the bar and looked straight into the eyes of the trembling baritone. "Do not worry, Pasquale," she said sweetly. "I am not going to hit you."

Amato and Caruso exchanged an uneasy glance. They went on. The next time Emmy sang with Amato, she deliberately sang her part a half-tone sharp— with the result that Amato was made to sound flat.

That was what did it. That was what finally caused the explosion in the orchestra pit. Toscanini simply blew up. The conductor outdid himself. Such an outpouring of invective and sarcasm and vitriol the Metropolitan had never heard before. Toscanini was democratic in his condemnation; he denounced singers, orchestra, stagehands, Gatti-Casazza, and the President of the United States alike.

Getting bawled out by Arturo Toscanini was never a pleasant experience, but just the same Caruso breathed a small sigh of relief. This was the old Toscanini they all knew and loved! That other Toscanini— the kind, patient one— was a stranger. With a yelling Maestro, Caruso always knew where he stood.

Toscanini called them imbeciles and ignoramuses and— worst of all— *amateurs*. Emmy Destinn, whose deliberate off-key singing had proved the final straw, stood impervious to the barrage of fiery abuse emanating from the pit. Gatti-Casazza was on the stage, trying to calm the conductor down. But Toscanini wouldn't be calmed. He broke his baton in two, hurled the pieces at the stage, and turned on his heel and stomped out.

"I think rehearsal is over for today," Amato said shakily.

Belasco was again dabbing at his forehead with his handkerchief. "Do you think the audience will stay for the second act?" he asked no one in particular.

Gatti-Casazza was looking at his watch. "Well, it is getting late—almost time to quit anyway. Oh, dear!" he lamented, pulling at his beard. "I hope he comes back tomorrow!"

"Of course he will, Mr. Gatti," Caruso said. "The Maestro always comes back."

The general manager didn't look so sure. "I've never seen him this angry before."

"Because he has been keeping it held in for so long. Like a pressure valve building up steam inside a bottle cork." Caruso knew that wasn't right but couldn't figure out how to fix it.

"He gave me his word," Gatti-Casazza

complained. "He promised me he would not lose his temper even once while we rehearse *Fanciulla.*"

"He did?" Caruso was surprised. "Why would he make a promise like that?"

"Because I asked him to." Gatti-Casazza glanced over to where Puccini was standing and lowered his voice. "Out of consideration for our composer and his troubles. You understand."

So that was why Toscanini had been such a sweetheart up until now. Because Mr. Gatti had made him promise to behave, the same way he'd made Caruso promise. "Perhaps it was too much to ask," the tenor suggested.

Everyone was leaving—rather rapidly, in fact. The usual cheery goodbyes were missing. Nobody invited anybody to dinner.

Caruso hurried the two short blocks to the Hotel Knickerbocker. Even before his bath and massage, he called Ugo into his bedroom for a private talk. "I have decided upon a course of action," he announced, "and I need your help."

Ugo sat down, all eager attention. "What do I do?"

"The police are keeping it secret that

Davila was blackmailing Puccini, at least until the inquest. The only other ones who know about it are you and I." Caruso thought it best not to mention that he himself had spilled the beans to Pasquale Amato. "Since the police think Puccini killed Davila and *we* know he did not," stressing the *we*, "then it is up to us to find the real killer."

Caruso's emphasis on the pronoun didn't work. "Are you so sure Mr. Puccini is innocent, Rico?" Ugo asked. "You want him to be innocent, but—"

"He *is* innocent, and we will have no more talk about it! Do you understand?"

"Yes, Rico," Ugo sighed.

"So. Now if Puccini did not kill him, then someone else did. Correct?"

"Yes, Rico."

"So who is this somebody? Another blackmail victim! Correct?"

Ugo looked dubious.

Caruso scowled at him. "Why no 'Yes, Rico'? Can there not be another blackmail victim? Or two? Or a dozen?"

The valet began to look interested. "A whole lot of people?"

"Why not? Luigi Davila may have forged

many other letters besides the ones Elvira Puccini is supposed to have written."

Ugo thought about that. "Then why do the police not find these other letters when they search Luigi Davila's office?"

"Aha!" Caruso pounced. "Because the killer takes all the other letters away with him after he kills Davila!"

"All but Elvira Puccini's?"

"All but those. Perhaps he overlooks them, perhaps he leaves them behind on purpose. To throw suspicion on Puccini." Caruso sat back in his chair, pleased with his line of reasoning. "Well? What do you think?"

Ugo mulled it over a long time; then a slow smile began to spread over his face. "I think you are a very smart man, Rico! So what do we do now?"

"I want you to start asking questions among the other valets and the stagehands at the opera house. But do it subtly. Listen to conversations, try to find out if anyone knows of a dark secret in somebody's past. See if you can discover anyone who might be vulnerable to blackmail. Servants know these things, and they like to talk about them, yes? The stagehands might know something, but concentrate on the other personal servants. Do you understand?"

Ugo nodded eagerly, pleased with his assignment. "And you, Rico? What do you do?"

"I do the same as you, but I do it with the other people at the opera house." He considered a moment. "And I think I start with that very strange man, Mr. David Belasco."

EIGHT

DAVID BELASCO HAD risen early. He'd been neglecting his own work of late; that musical madhouse at Broadway and Thirty-ninth had been taking up all his attention as well as most of his time. Not that he would have had it any other way.

The Girl of the Golden West was not the first of his plays Puccini had turned into opera; there'd also been *Madame Butterfly*. But *Butterfly*-the-opera had premièred in Italy, and Belasco had had no say in its staging—although he'd worked on later productions in London and New York. But now with a world première only a few days away, he could no more stay away from the Metropolitan Opera House than he could do without eating.

He sat at his desk in his private rooms

at the new theatre he had built and named after himself. Box-office receipts for *The Concert* were holding up well, and his new production at the Hudson Theatre — *Nobody's Widow*, starring his best actress, Blanche Bates — showed signs of settling in for a good run. *The Return of Peter Grimm* would be opening at the Hollis Street Theatre in Boston next month. He should be writing, though; he found a new French play he thought he could adapt to the American stage without too much difficulty. But that would have to wait until after the end of the year.

Belasco studied the new contract Blanche Bates was insisting upon. Blanche had created the title role in the original *Girl of the Golden West,* and now was demanding the moon and the stars. But as long as she continued drawing audiences into the Hudson Theatre, Belasco would give her what she wanted. Within reason, of course. All actors were children, not really knowing what was good for them. But if actors were children, then opera singers were *babies.* Naive and selfish, but ultimately controllable.

He thought of the opera's three leads and

laughed to himself. Only Pasquale Amato looked the part he played. But Enrico Caruso and Emmy Destinn—what an unlikely romantic couple those two made! They were both a little too old and a great deal too heavy for their roles—especially Caruso, who needed to lose a good fifty pounds. But on the operatic stage appearance didn't seem to count for much; it was only the voice that mattered. Belasco didn't see why opera should not have both, and had bent all his effort toward creating a semblance of reality on stage.

But the illusion of reality was hard to maintain with a practical joker like Caruso on the loose. Belasco had said nothing at the time, but he'd been shocked when the prank came to light—gluing the pages of the Bible together! The trick was close to sacrilege; one simply did not treat the Holy Book in so disrespectful a manner. Belasco himself was always careful never even to lay another book on top of the Bible.

Yet really, he told himself, that was only a minor distraction. The one big problem remaining was that *chorus*. An unruly bunch, hard to tame; but they were at last beginning to show some restraint. By the time of the première, they might even be doing it right. But in one area of endeavor Belasco had to admit total defeat; he'd failed to teach even one member of the cast how to throw a lasso.

He got up from the desk and walked through the rooms just for the emotional support his surroundings gave him. His own private stage setting. A feast for the eye, a mélange of objets d'art and antiquarian curiosities intermingled with stage properties from his own theatrical productions. This glorious disarray seldom failed to disconcert the first-time visitor. Belasco didn't mind; he never objected to anything that put him at an advantage. Visitors— and Belasco did not admit many— often became disoriented in the maze-like arrangement of shelf after shelf of books and collectors' treasures. And in a suite filled with so much richness and so much busyness, the visitor's eye was naturally drawn to the one clean-lined, austere thing in the place: himself. Belasco knew well the value of playing against one's backdrop.

He stood in front of a full-length mirror in a gilt rococo frame and examined himself critically. The brown eyes were clear, the skin tone was holding up. The silver, sculpted hair looked better than his young-man's hair had looked. A thickening at the waist was adequately concealed by the ecclesiastical garb he wore. He was still a striking figure, and he knew it. He also knew how to use his appearance and his voice and his mannerisms to create the effect he wanted.

David Belasco was acting a part. He didn't know how *not* to act a part. Even when he was alone, as now, he kept in character most of the time. He'd been accused of posturing once or twice, but he'd brushed the accusations aside. The role he wanted to create was that of a civilized, soft-spoken, wise, self-possessed man of Absolute Authority. A judge to be appealed to. A leader whose orders are followed without question. Belasco liked getting his own way.

Everyone connected with the theatre — both the legitimate stage and the operatic stage — made a habit of acting offstage as well as on; but few could perform as well as David Belasco. One who came close, Belasco felt, was Arturo Toscanini. Belasco liked Toscanini; he'd sensed a kindred spirit there. He admired the other man's professionalism, his sensitivity to the music he was conducting, his exercise of authority.

From the very first rehearsal Belasco had attended, he'd felt that Toscanini too had been acting a part: that of the kindly, understanding father. But while the conductor was calm on the outside, he'd been burning inwardly. So much temperament and passion, kept bottled up like that! But Toscanini had been unable to sustain his role, and the result was the terrible eruption yesterday that had ended the rehearsal prematurely. Belasco's own control, however, had never slipped, even though he'd been sorely tried at times. Unlike the conductor, *he* was still in character.

Belasco was feeling good.

He ran his hand down one silken panel of a folding oriental screen, enjoying its touch. He'd placed the screen in front of a window seat where he could see without being seen, where he could sit and look out on the world— or at least that part of it that passed by the Belasco Theatre on West Forty-fourth Street. He liked watching the variety of people coming and going beneath his high perch. They were there to be examined.

One in particular caught his eye. Lantern-jawed, corpulent, ridiculously overdressed. What was Caruso doing here? Belasco stared down at the top of the singer's curly-brimmed hat as the other man entered the theatre.

Belasco sat behind his oriental screen and waited for the knock at the door. And waited. And waited. Then he heard the sound of the door handle being turned. The faintest of clicks reached his ear. The door had been opened.

He looked cautiously around the edge of the screen. There stood Caruso in the entryway, his eyes saucer-sized and his mouth hanging open as he took in his surroundings. Amazement, confusion, admiration, uneasiness, and awe passed in turn across his face as he gazed at all the heaped-up beauty of Belasco's rooms.

Belasco smothered a laugh. Was it the Italian temperament to show everything one was feeling, or was it just Caruso's particular childlike nature? In a moment he would step forward and demand to know why the singer had entered his private rooms without knocking; but for the time being he was enjoying Caruso's disorientation too much to reveal his presence.

Caruso didn't seem to know what to look at first. He cooed and clucked over Belasco's collection of precious glass. Then he was distracted by a model of the stage setting for *The Rose of the Rancho*. He looked briefly into the alcove stocked with relics associated with Napoleon – including a lock of the Emperor's hair. Then he moved off among the maze of shelves. Belasco remembered that Caruso was said to be something of a collector himself; curious, he followed his uninvited visitor.

Caruso stopped to examine the two dozen different types of daggers he found on display. A chair once used by England's Henry VIII elicited a long and appreciative *ahhhh*. The singer avoided a sinister-looking set of black armor and bumped a secret spring with his elbow; a wall panel raised to reveal a lighted recess filled with jeweled rosaries.

The tenor moved on, trying to take in everything at once. He had trouble tearing himself away from a hearth made of tiles stolen from the Alhambra by slaves who'd labored there. He opened a low Gothic door and peered into a tunnel filled with rare pamphlets. He rounded a corner and exclaimed with startled delight— he'd come upon a small fountain flinging its spray over a pool in which violets, sweet peas, and roses were floating.

But then Caruso abruptly jerked himself into an almost military posture and made a gesture that seemed to reject all the things he so obviously wanted to linger over. Resolutely he marched back to the desk— where he started going through Belasco's papers!

Belasco watched in amazement for two full minutes. When Caruso didn't find anything of interest on the top of the desk, he started opening the drawers to see what was there. Belasco stepped into view, lowered his voice an octave, and said in his best King Lear manner: "What is the meaning of this, sir?"

Caruso jumped a foot. "Oh, ah, uh, Mr. Belasco! Uh, I did not know you were here!"

"Obviously," Belasco said in a way that made Caruso's hair rise.

"I knock," the tenor said hastily. "I knock but—"

"You did not knock," Belasco interrupted coldly. "I was here all the time. And you did not knock. You sneaked in— "

"I do not sneak!" Caruso's outrage was almost authentic. "I sometimes move quietly, but I never sneak!"

"What do you want, Mr. Caruso? Why were you going through my papers?"

"Papers, uh, that is a mistake. Uh, I hear about your marvelous collection and I want to, uh." He looked around desperately. "I want to see this!" He grabbed up a Japanese sword.

Belasco blinked. "That is a stage property from *The Darling of the Gods.*"

Caruso hastily put the sword down. "I mean this!" He seized a small figurine of Hercules.

"Yes, I can see how you might confuse the two," Belasco said dryly.

Caruso started backing toward the door. "I come at a bad time— I am so sorry. I interrupt you. So many lovely things!"

Belasco followed him, saying nothing but looking icicles.

Caruso, on the other hand, was sweating buckets. "Someday you must come see my collection. We compare, yes?" His hand found the door handle behind him. "So nice to see you— good day!"

"Mr. Caruso!" An iceberg speaking.

The tenor wilted. "Yes?"

"My Hercules?"

Caruso thrust the figurine into Belasco's outstretched hands, opened the door, and fled.

"Yes, we are doubling the price of admission," Gatti-Casazza was saying on the telephone. "But that is only for the première, you understand." He listened a moment to the gentleman from *The New York Times* on the other end of the line. "No, I do not know what the scalpers are getting . . . what's that? . . . Thirty times the box-office price! That's outrageous."

Secretly, Mr. Gatti was pleased; scalpers' prices were the most reliable indicator of public interest that he knew. And he did not tell the reporter that if the première was a success, he was planning to *quadruple* the admission prices for the second performance.

He brought the conversation to an end and hung up, satisfied. Two days until dress rehearsal! The opera was coming along nicely; now that Toscanini had had his temper tantrum and Caruso had played his practical joke, there should be no more high jinks.

A slight movement in the open doorway of his office caught his attention. He looked up to see one eye peering at him around the doorframe. "Yes?" he said sharply.

An embarrassed Enrico Caruso stepped into view. "Uh, good morning, Mr. Gatti. I come to see how you are feeling today."

"I am well, Enrico, thank you," Gatti-Casazza answered, puzzled.

"That is good," the tenor smiled, and left.

The general manager shrugged and got back to work. A note from the printer, saying the programs were ready— good. Mr. Gatti approved payment of a few bills. The bleachers still had to be put up at the carriage entrance on Thirty-ninth Street; the press needed a place to stand where they could note who came through and what they were wearing. He telephoned the florist to find out what time of day the curtain-call bouquets for *Fanciulla's* three principals would be delivered. Then he read a memo from the house manager— oh dear, the plumbing again! He'd better see what that was all about.

He found the plumbers at work in the gentlemen's washroom backstage. "How bad is it this time?" he asked the man who seemed to be in charge.

"Not so bad," the man answered. "Coupla pipe fittings need replacing, thass all. We hadda turn the water off."

"How long will it take?"

"Twenty, thirty minutes."

Two hours, Gatti-Casazza thought. "I would appreciate haste on your part. We have a rehearsal here this afternoon."

"Haste makes waste," the plumber replied sententiously.

"Does it really? Well, do the best you can." He left the washroom—and found Caruso flattened against the wall outside the door, a foolish look on his face. "Enrico? If you want to use the washroom, I'm afraid the water will be off for a while."

"I can wait, I can wait," the tenor muttered and hastened away.

Gatti-Casazza checked his watch; if he hurried, he could squeeze in a visit to the silversmith before rehearsal started. That was one job he didn't want to delegate.

The December wind cut through him as

he hurried east on Fortieth Street, turned left on Fifth Avenue past the new Public Library, bucked the wind for another block until he came to the establishment of E. Klein and Sons, Silversmiths. Mr. Klein greeted him personally.

"Is it finished?" Gatti-Casazza asked eagerly.

"It is finished," Mr. Klein beamed. "Wait— I show you." He disappeared into the back room of his shop and reappeared carrying a folded black velvet cloth, which he opened ceremoniously to reveal an ornate silver wreath.

"Oh, Mr. Klein! It is beautiful!" Gatti-Casazza rotated the wreath in his hands, looking at it from all angles. "Truly beautiful! Oh, yes! I must congratulate you on an exquisite piece of workmanship!"

"You are satisfied?"

"I am more than satisfied, I am delighted! Mr. Puccini will adore it!" The general manager was planning to present the wreath to the composer between Acts II and III of the *Fanciulla* première, and it was to be a surprise; Gatti-Casazza worried about keeping it secret. "You have told no one?"

"Only my son Abraham knows," Mr.

Klein said. "He did part of the work. Do not worry, Mr. Gee Cee, Abraham is a good boy—he will not speak of the wreath."

Gatti-Casazza nodded. "And you will deliver it on the tenth? It must be the tenth—I do not want to have to hide it before then, and even one day later will be too late."

"At eleven o'clock on Saturday morning, the tenth of December," the silversmith intoned solemnly, "I personally will place the wreath in your hands." Suddenly he started, and hastily wrapped the wreath back up in the velvet cloth. "Someone is looking!"

Gatti-Casazza glanced over his shoulder —and saw Caruso out on the street, hands cupped around his eyes, peering through the shop window. In two strides the general manager was at the entrance; he pulled the door open angrily. "Enrico! What are you doing here?"

"I, uh . . . I start my Christmas shopping! Yes! I look for silver cuff links. This is a nice place, yes?"

"What did you just see?"

"See?"

"Yes, Enrico, *see.* What did you just see?"

Caruso shrugged. "I see you looking at a

kind of wreath."

Gatti-Casazza groaned. "You must mention this to no one." He told Mr. Klein goodbye and started walking Caruso back to the Metropolitan. He explained what the wreath was for, and urged the tenor to secrecy.

"Of course!" Caruso agreed enthusiastically. "What a wonderful gesture! Puccini will be enchanted. Do not worry, I tell no one. Mom's the word." He was quiet a moment, thinking. "Do you know, Mr. Gatti, our friend Belasco has worked very hard on *Fanciulla*. Perhaps some token for him, too? To let him know how much we appreciate all his effort?"

Gatti-Casazza groaned. "You must mention this to no one." He told Mr. Klein goodbye and started walking Caruso back to the Metropolitan. He explained what the wreath was for, and urged the tenor to secrecy.

Caruso waved a hand airily. "Piece of *torta*."

They were almost back to the Metropolitan when Gatti-Casazza thought of something. "Enrico—you were at the opera house when I left. Did you follow me to Mr. Klein's?"

"I? Follow you?" Caruso appeared astonished. "Why would I follow you? I am Christmas shopping early this year, that is all."

The general manager eyed him suspiciously but said no more. In the Met lobby they parted; Gatti-Casazza hurried up the stairway to his office.

To find Pasquale Amato waiting for him there. "Ah, Mr. Gatti—I come to beg. I desperately need two more guest tickets to the première. I promise them long ago, but—alas!—I do not have enough of my own."

The general manager shrugged out of his overcoat and sat at his desk. "I am sorry, Pasquale—there are no more tickets available."

"Perhaps just one?"

"Not even one. I am sorry."

The baritone sighed. "I was afraid of that. But always there is someone unable to come at the last minute. If I could have *those* tickets . . . ?"

Gatti-Casazza pulled at his beard. "Perhaps. Well, I shall speak to the box-office chief—we will see what can be done."

Amato bounded up out of his chair. "Thank you! I am eternally in your debt, dear Mr. Gatti!" The manager waved a hand at him as he left— and then heard a muffled sound from outside the door. "Oof!" came Amato's voice. "Sorry, Rico— I did not see you standing there."

Gatti-Casazza jumped up from his desk and hurried to the door, just in time to catch a glimpse of the broad back of his star tenor, beating a hasty retreat down the stairway.

Emmy Destinn sat in her dressing room, frowning as she read a letter from home.

Sigrid came in, carrying the soprano's *Fanciulla* costume. "Bad news?"

"Gunfire in the streets of Prague again." She folded the letter and put it away. "Ever since I was a little girl— they fight. They fight, then they sign a treaty not to fight, and then they fight some more."

Sigrid laid a sympathetic hand on Emmy's arm. "It will stop some day. And you are safe here." She put up an ironing board and started pressing the soprano's costume.

Emmy was troubled. The shaky Austro-Hungarian Empire was obviously trying to hold itself together by whatever means possible and at whatever cost. Time and again the Austrians had put down the Czech rebels, but the movement simply would not die. Slavs deserved their own federation! Emmy had long since given up trying to keep track of the various factions involved in the fighting; what she knew for a certainty was that her section of Europe had not known true stability once during her entire lifetime.

You are safe here, Sigrid had said. Not for the first time, Emmy wondered what was involved in becoming a citizen of the United States of America. She was a little awed by her own daring; she'd never even been to this country until two years ago. And Prague was home—beautiful Prague, with its big house she'd filled with antiques and cats and friends. On the other hand, there was a great deal to be said for waking up in the morning knowing that an armed force from New Jersey would not be invading Manhattan that day.

She watched her maid at the ironing board. "Sigrid—do you miss Sweden?"

"I miss Stockholm," Sigrid said without hesitation. "The rest of the country, you can have.''

Emmy smiled; Sigrid would be no problem. She'd come with her wherever she decided to live—unless it was Italy. Sigrid didn't like Italy. Her maid had had to learn the language, since Italian was the international speech of opera. But she'd once dismissed the entire country as ''heat, dust, loud voices, and bad manners.'' Poor Sigrid! A great deal of her life was spent backstage at the various opera houses of the world; but no matter which opera house it was, she was always surrounded by volatile Italians. No wonder she got what the Americans called ''peckish'' once in a while.

The soprano touched her jaw. If she moved it just right—here!—she could still feel a twinge from the poke she'd taken yesterday. She was beginning to regret walloping Pasquale Amato so hard; she'd simply taken out on him all the frustrations aroused by that ill-fated rehearsal. But she would not apologize to the baritone—no indeed! Let him stay intimidated. It might teach him to be more careful.

''Does your jaw still hurt?'' Sigrid asked sympathetically.

Emmy put on a fairly good martyred look.

"I try not to think about it. Sigrid, if you iron that skirt much longer you're going to wear a hole in it!"

"You must look nice," the maid said in a no-argument voice.

"Mr. Belasco doesn't think so," the soprano grumbled. "He wants me to look dowdy. Cotton stockings!"

"He does not mean that, surely."

"He *does* mean that, surely."

Sigrid shook her head, not convinced. "Such a nice man—so polite and well-spoken. He will not make you wear something you do not wish to wear."

"You deceive yourself. That mild manner is just a face Mr. Belasco presents to the world. Underneath is a will of iron."

Sigrid was finished. She put the costume on a padded hanger and held it up for inspection. Both women stared at it in distaste. A plain white long-sleeved blouse, and a floor-length corduroy skirt. A far cry from the silks and satins of *Tosca* and *Butterfly* or the exotic garb of *Aïda*.

Sigrid gave that half-sniff, half-tsk that only the Scandinavians can manage and took the costume over to the wardrobe cabinet—which wouldn't open. Each time Sigrid pulled the handle, the door would give maybe an inch and then snap back. "I can't get it open— it's caught on something."

Emmy went over to help. She gave the wardrobe door a hard jerk and it flew open— to reveal Enrico Caruso crowded in among the dresses, grinning fatuously, embarrassed to death at being caught.

Sigrid squawked and dropped the carefully pressed costume while Emmy stared open-mouthed. "Rico! What are you doing there?" the soprano demanded.

Sheepishly he held up a cigarette. "Looking for a match?"

"Get out of there, you foolish man!" Emmy said angrily. "Get out at once! I want an explanation, Rico!"

Awkwardly the tenor stepped out of the wardrobe cabinet. A flood of high-pitched, unintelligible Swedish assailed his ears; then Sigrid realized he didn't understand what she was saying and switched to Italian. "So! Now you hide yourself in wardrobe cabinets where you can peek out at the ladies when they are not looking!"

"I? Peek? I never peek!" Caruso proclaimed indignantly.

"Peeping Tommaso! Spying on innocent ladies!"

"How can I spy? There are no peepholes in the cabinet! See for yourself!" He gestured grandly at the wardrobe and started inching toward the dressing-room door.

Sigrid inspected the wardrobe cabinet for cracks or holes. She found none but refused to be mollified. "Look at Madame's dresses! You have crushed them! Now I will have to press everything again!"

"Rico," Emmy said curiously, "when did you take up eavesdropping as a hobby?"

Caruso bolted through the door.

Toscanini muttered to himself as he paced up and down one of the side aisles of the Met's auditorium. He was not satisfied with the chorus of tenors that hummed offstage in accompaniment to the soprano-tenor duet in the first act. Their attack was smooth and the various voices blended nicely—but the result was curiously empty, not nearly sensuous enough. More work was needed there.

The duet itself was exquisite; Destinn and Caruso got better every time they sang it. But the duet—*all* the duets in *Fanciulla*, in fact—might cause a problem for American audiences. These duets were different from what the Americans were used to; they were duologues, actually—the soloists taking turns singing, the two voices uniting only toward the end. Well, Toscanini thought, the Americans would just have to learn to appreciate the beauties of the verismo duet and it was up to him to teach them!

Puccini had mentioned he thought Emmy Destinn lacked energy in her performance; he obviously wanted a strong heroine in this opera, a change from the ultra-fragile heroine of *Butterfly*. But Toscanini had reassured the composer that Destinn always started slowly and built gradually to a performance peak. The night of the première she would sing with the same soaring urgency she brought to the role of Aïda. No problem there.

Toscanini stopped his pacing. Surely the plumbers were finished by now? He directed his steps toward the gentlemen's washroom backstage.

The bass singing the Wells Fargo agent and the tenor singing the bartender were both beginning to push a little—trying to make their small roles larger. He'd have to put a stop to that. But Toscanini could understand their eagerness; the music

188

invited that sort of pushing. No other score of Puccini's was punctuated with so many markings for excessive dynamics— *allegro brutale, allegro feroce.* And he couldn't think of another opera score in which the word *tutti* appeared so frequently: all the instruments of the orchestra playing together at the same time. The result was a massive, primitive sound that the conductor found tremendously exciting.

When it was done right. How that orchestra infuriated him! Parts of it, at any rate— the woodwinds, for instance. Puccini had orchestrated for a much larger woodwind section than usual, and they had had to hire extra musicians. *Musicians*— bah! Not one of those newcomers was able to tease out the best tone his instrument was capable of producing. How many times had he told Gatti-Casazza, you simply cannot expect a first-rate orchestral sound from second-rate musicians! But no, the penny-pinching general manager went right on hiring any low-priced hack he could find—

Toscanini stopped himself. His breath was short and his face flushed; he was doing it again. He fumbled something out of his coat pocket and made himself focus his attention on it. A few minutes of forced concentration did the truck and left him calm once more. The conductor heaved a sigh of relief; his temper had almost gotten away from him again. He went into the washroom.

No one was there. Had the plumbers finished or just quit work for the day? He tried a faucet— ah, the water was back on. Toscanini took off his coat and fastidiously hung it up before going into one of the stalls.

Quietly, stealthily, Enrico Caruso tiptoed into the washroom, keeping one eye on the closed door of the stall. He felt in Toscanini's coat pocket; his fingers closed around an object made of metal and glass. Carefully he took it out.

And almost dropped it in his surprise. *Per dio!* It was a— what did they call it?— a Bughouse puzzle! Bughouse, yes. A glass-covered box marked off into little compartments, with bits of lead that had to be fitted into the proper places entirely by external manipulation. Bughouse puzzle— a child's toy.

Caruso put the puzzle back in Toscanini's coat pocket and tiptoed out of the washroom.

At last, Toscanini was satisfied with Act II. Caruso would not be needed immediately in the third act, so he hurried up the stairs to his dressing room and shut the door. He sank into a chair and buried his head in his hands. What a day!

He'd certainly be glad when *this* rehearsal was over. David Belasco had cut him dead when they'd met backstage. Mr. Gatti had followed him everywhere, watching every move he made. And in the part of Act II where he was seated at a table, Emmy Destinn had clamped a strong hand on his shoulder to prevent his escape— and proceeded to sing full voice directly into his left ear. His head was still ringing.

Only Toscanini had been in a good mood; he could afford to relax a little, he'd had his breakdown. And if the biggest secret in the conductor's life was that he liked to play with a Bughouse puzzle, then Caruso could cross him off the list of suspects. *List.* That's what he should do— make a list. And notes. Detectives always kept notes.

He moved over to his writing table, but found he was out of paper. The tenor made a sound of exasperation. How could he make notes if he had nothing to write on? He distinctly remembered telling Martino to get more writing paper— no, that was not precisely true. He distinctly remembered *meaning* to tell Martino. Ah well, he would borrow some of Pasquale's. The baritone was on stage at the moment, but he would not mind if Caruso helped himself.

The tenor found what he was looking for in a drawer of Amato's make-up table. He found something else as well: at the back of the drawer was a single letter, addressed to the baritone in a slanting feminine handwriting. A billet-doux? *A good detective checks everything,* Caruso thought gleefully, and took the letter out of the envelope.

My beloved husband—
I long for the day you return to
our warm bed in our cozy house in
Milan. . . .

Milan? Caruso frowned. Amato's home and family were in Salerno.

We have an anniversary to celebrate,
my dearest one. Soon it will be exactly

two years since you and I were first
united in holy matrimony. . . .

Two years? Amato had been married a lot longer than that. A horrible suspicion crept into Caruso's mind— quickly he checked the signature.

> *Your loving and faithful wife,*
> *Francesca*

Caruso let out a *Pagliacci* sob; Amato's wife was named Rosa. After a moment he went on with the letter.

I think of you there in New York surrounded by beautiful women and my heart breaks. Pasquale, my love! Hurry home to me. I have made plans for the celebration of our anniversary. . . .

Caruso felt his face turning red as he read the woman's graphically detailed description of exactly *how* she planned to celebrate. He stopped and fanned himself with the letter. Then he went back and read the good parts again.

Finally he folded the letter carefully and

replaced it where he'd found it. Who was Francesca? Some lusty young thing Pasquale Amato had deceived into "marriage" by neglecting to mention he already had a wife? Poor Francesca! Poor Rosa! Caruso felt pity for both the women who called themselves Pasquale's wife.

And poor Enrico! How was he going to cope with this horrible knowledge, this unwanted news that one of his oldest and dearest friends was a bigamist?

NINE

MARTINO UNCORKED A bottle of witch hazel and poured some of the liquid onto a wad of cotton. "Close your eyes."

Caruso obeyed. His face was still pink from the medicated steam he'd been breathing that nevertheless had failed to relieve his headache. Martino dabbed the tenor's forehead with the witch hazel, being careful not to let any drip on Caruso's green-and-gold satin robe. The cool liquid evaporated almost immediately. "More," said Caruso.

But Martino had to cease his ministrations momentarily; someone was at the door. It was Martino's job to turn away, tactfully, the dozens of uninvited visitors who called on Caruso almost daily. In the next room the telephone was ringing; Caruso could

195

hear Mario saying, "He is not well and cannot be disturbed." The young valet's mournful manner of speaking made it sound as if the tenor were on his deathbed.

Martino returned carrying an empty calling-card tray. "A man with a painting to sell – wrapped in brown paper and tied with string. He would not leave his name or identify the painting."

"Ah, *dio!* It is probably stolen." A lot of thieves had found their way to Caruso's door once it became known the tenor collected objets d'art.

"I tell him we are not buying paintings this year."

The witch-hazel treatment didn't really help; Caruso waved Martino away. After sitting quietly and feeling sorry for himself a few minutes, the tenor took out his sketch pad and began to draw. A few bold lines, a squiggle here and there, curves to mark the plumpness of the cheeks – and a fair likeness of Luigi Davila looked back at him.

"His nose was a little longer," Martino said from behind Caruso's shoulder.

Caruso lengthened the nose – yes, that was right. That was what the dead man had looked like. He tore off the sheet and started a new sketch. Dark hair just covering the tops of the ears but long in back, penetrating black eyes, drooping black mustache. Pasquale Amato to the life. Caruso placed the two sketches side by side and stared at them. His headache grew worse.

Pasquale didn't even know Luigi Davila — he'd had to ask Caruso who he was! Unbidden, a thought from nowhere: *He could have been pretending.*

No, it was absurd! Even more absurd than Lieutenant O'Halloran's thinking Puccini was the murderer. Pasquale Amato was a *friend;* friends were not murderers. Especially not this friend— a more stable, humane, rational man Caruso had never met. They'd known each other for so long, they had worked and played together so often— how could he think for one moment that Pasquale could be a killer?

A man with two wives makes a good target for blackmail.

How odd: Amato's role in *Fanciulla* was that of a lustful man trying to persuade a girl to marry him even though he already had a wife. Caruso wondered how his friend managed to keep Rosa and Francesca from finding out about each other—that must take some doing! Abruptly the thought occurred to him that he must stop thinking like a friend and look at the problem the way a *detective* would. Impartially. Objectively. Other-ly.

Pasquale Amato had known Puccini was being blackmailed because Caruso himself had told him so. If Pasquale were also a blackmail victim, he would welcome the news about Puccini—because that meant he could get rid of his blackmailer and throw suspicion on the composer. As long as he thought he was Davila's only victim, he would hesitate to act. But when some big-mouthed tenor comes along and gives away Puccini's secret, then the hesitation might disappear.

Yes. That is the way a real detective would see it.

There were other little things, vague and inconclusive. Pasquale had never really tried to help Puccini. In fact, he'd done his best to discourage Caruso from investigating on his own. *Don't meddle,* he'd said. That could just be the conservative approach of a basically sensible man. Or it could be the caution of a killer who didn't want a friend to find out the truth about him.

Caruso walked over to the window and looked down on Times Square. The weather was vile—snow and rain, high winds and low temperatures. Past the Times Tower on West Forty-second Street Caruso could just make out the entrance of David Belasco's old theatre, the Republic. That was where it had all begun; it was there Puccini first saw *The Girl of the Golden West*.

It was late afternoon. The day's rehearsal had been shorter than usual. They'd had to vacate the stage because that night's performance was scheduled to begin earlier than the Metropolitan's usual eight-o'clock curtain; *Fanciulla* had gotten short shrift so *Die Walküre* could thunder away on the main stage. But in a little while Caruso would be going to meet Amato and Emmy Destinn at Del Pezzo's Restaurant. Pasquale had invited Emmy, to reestablish the good feelings that had been rather seriously strained by that one disastrous rehearsal. He wanted Caruso along as a buffer.

Today was Wednesday, and tomorrow was dress rehearsal. Friday's calls would depend upon how dress rehearsal went. The Saturday matinee was *Faust*, and Saturday night was the world première of *La Fanciulla del West*. Following the performance, the Vanderbilts—ah yes, the Vanderbilts—were hosting a supper party and reception. That should keep them up most of the night; Sunday would be spent recuperating.

And Monday was the inquest into the death of Luigi Davila.

Lieutenant O'Halloran—if he knew there was someone else who might have a motive for killing Davila, surely he would see to it that Puccini was not arrested? Two possible murderers, with no real proof that either man was guilty. In Italy, the authorities would simply arrest both men. Caruso did not think it was the same here.

But could he take that chance? Just telling O'Halloran about the bigamy—that would cost him Pasquale's friendship for life, even if the baritone was never charged with the crime of murder. Caruso felt he was being forced to decide between the two men, Puccini and Amato. How could anyone make such a choice? Pasquale was more than just a friend—*per dio,* he *loved* the man! He had never been that close to Puccini; only recently had they become friends.

But it wasn't that simple. Puccini was one of the greatest composers Italy had ever produced. The man had more music in him, more opera to write — how could Caruso risk all that glory being lost to the world? Puccini's name would be remembered long after Caruso's and Amato's were forgotten. One does not throw away a creative genius so easily.

Caruso stood by the window a long time, remembering details of his long association with Amato. The horseplay on stage, the serious moments of creating beautiful music, the supper parties, the after-hours escapades — *No!* he decided suddenly and emphatically. He could never turn in his friend. He was appalled with himself for having even considered it. Caruso resolved then and there he would never reveal Amato's guilty secret to another living soul. Never, never, never, never, *never*.

Abruptly he whirled from the window and hurried over to the table where he'd left the two sketches. He picked them up and stared at them a moment. Then he angrily tore both sketches to bits and threw the pieces away.

Never.

Caruso pushed open the door of Del Pezzo's Restaurant on West Thirty-fourth Street to be met by a wave of laughter and warmth, as well as the most delicious cooking aromas he had ever smelled. Ah, how he loved restaurants! Caruso spent so many hours in restaurants he'd come to look upon them as a sort of second home. Good food remained one of the pure, unadulterated joys of life, regardless of what else might go wrong. His mouth was watering in anticipation, and already his headache seemed better.

Caruso was greeted by Del Pezzo himself, an old friend who was always glad to see him. "Ah, Enrico, we have been waiting for you! I take your coat, yes?"

The tenor handed over his coat, hat, muffler, gloves, and cane. "My friends are here?"

"They are here and so hungry they have already ordered. What do your taste buds cry out for tonight?"

"Clams and spaghetti," Caruso said without hesitation. "And later — zabaglione."

Del Pezzo led him through rows of tables covered with checkered cloths to one where

Emmy Destinn and Pasquale Amato were sitting. Caruso was cheered to see they were laughing and talking easily; that was good, everyone should be friends.

"Ah, Rico, old friend—we have been waiting for you!" Amato called out. "That is your chair there."

Caruso sat down. "All is well?"

"Quite well," Emmy said lightly. "We have decided to forgive each other."

"We have also agreed never to mention that dreadful rehearsal again," Amato added. "I had more accidents that one afternoon than in all the other rehearsals I have ever done! One thing after another."

"And *your* accidents have a way of spilling over onto other people," Emmy contributed, also forgetting they'd agreed not to talk about it. "Not to mention the unnecessary complications added by a certain practical joker in our midst." She glared at Caruso with mock ferociousness.

"The Bible," Caruso groaned. "But I do not glue those pages together! Something happens, everyone thinks I am responsible—but I do nothing!"

"Hah," Emmy snorted.

"He is telling the truth, Emmy," Amato

said, surprisingly. "Rico did not glue the Bible pages together. I did." The other two stared at him in astonishment. "It took me the *longest* time," Amato complained. "Every single page — a dab here, a dab there — "

"But, but why do you not say something at the time?" Caruso sputtered. "Why do you let everyone go on thinking I am the guilty one?"

"Because *that* is the joke, Rico. It is time you got a taste of your own medicine. The joke is not the Bible, but your getting blamed for it. The joke is on *you.*"

Caruso sat there speechless — but Emmy was laughing her head off. She reached across the table and patted Amato's hand. "You have redeemed yourself."

Just then the waiter arrived with a tray laden with spicy food. Emmy and Amato dug in with gusto; Caruso chewed a clam thoughtfully.

"Oh my, look at Rico," Emmy said after a few minutes. "He is pouting."

"I do not pout," the tenor said a touch waspishly. "I think seriously. But I never pout."

"Surely you are not angry, Rico?" Amato asked. "Do I get angry when you play a trick on me? No, I do not! Not ever."

"That is true," Caruso sighed. "You are right, Pasquale—I deserve it." Nevertheless, his feelings were hurt. Here he had just made this big decision never to reveal Amato's secret—only to find out his friend had made a goat of him.

"What are you thinking seriously about?" Emmy asked him.

"Friendship," he growled.

The other two burst out laughing. *"Cielo!"* Amato exclaimed. "Emmy, I ask Rico here to help me win back your friendship. But now I fear I must ask *your* help in convincing our sensitive friend here that I am not such a terrible villain after all."

"He is not such a terrible villain after all, Rico," Emmy said agreeably.

"Oh?" Caruso said sourly. "What kind of villain is he, then?" That launched a lively discussion of degrees of villainy, both on the stage and off, that Caruso eventually found himself joining in on. The three discovered they were in wild disagreement as to what constituted villainous behavior. With one exception.

"Luigi Davila was a villain of the very worst sort," Emmy pronounced decisively, while the two men nodded emphatic agreement. "A blackmailer must surely be the lowest form of life on the face of the earth."

"Did you know him, Emmy?" Caruso asked.

"I met him once. He wanted me to sign a contract with him."

"What happened?"

Emmy giggled. "I turned Sigrid loose on him. He never bothered me again."

"That would do it," Caruso agreed. "But what about the man who killed Davila? Where does he rank on our scale of villainy?"

There was silence. Then Amato remarked, "Perhaps I should not say so, but I do not think killing a blackmailer is the worst crime a man can commit. How else does one pry loose a leech? There is no satisfactory solution."

"Would you kill a blackmailer, Pasquale?" Caruso asked slyly.

Amato smiled. "Alas—no, I would not. Killing a man takes the heart of a lion, and I . . . I am a pussycat. I cannot kill."

And to his immense relief, Caruso found that he believed his friend with all his heart and soul. Pasquale Amato could not kill. No matter how many wives he had tucked away, he would not kill to protect that or any other secret. Violence was simply not a part of the man's nature.

By the time they reached the zabaglione and coffee, Caruso was back to his normal cheerful self. Nothing was so satisfying as the company of good friends following a good meal. The incident of the glued Bible still rankled a little, but the evening had produced one unexpected bonus: his headache was gone.

Caruso left Del Pezzo's feeling better in several ways than when he went in.

"Bath, Rico?" Martino greeted the tenor when he returned to the Hotel Knickerbocker.

"In just a few little moments. First I must speak to Ugo. Send him in here, please, Martino."

When he and Ugo were alone, Caruso plunged right in. "Tomorrow afternoon is dress rehearsal, Ugo—we are running out of time. Tell me, where have your investigations led you? Do any of the servants know of a secret scandal in their employers' lives?"

"Nothing that is not already general knowledge," Ugo said with barely concealed excitement. "But do not despair, Rico— I have found what you are looking for! Two of the servants themselves may be paying blackmail!"

"The servants themselves?" Caruso had never even considered that possibility. "Who are they?"

Ugo was grinning smugly. "The first is Sigrid— Madame Destinn's maid."

Caruso found himself grinning back; the thought that that impossible woman might be the villain he was pursuing pleased him enormously. "What terrible thing has Sigrid done?"

Ugo lowered his voice, even though they were alone. "It is said," he whispered, drawing it out, "that eight years ago she gave birth to an illegitimate child!"

Caruso was dumbfounded. "Sigrid? A *mother?!*"

Ugo nodded. "It is supposed to be a big secret, but three different valets tell me the story. And two of the stagehands know about it."

Caruso tried to digest this information; of all the women he knew, Sigrid seemed the *least* likely to succumb to passion and get herself involved in an illicit liaison. "I do not believe it," he said at last.

Ugo shrugged. "Every month she sends most of her salary to Stockholm— to support the child. A little girl, they say."

Sigrid, with a daughter! Caruso tried to picture Emmy's maid with a little girl and failed utterly. But Ugo had said three valets and two stagehands had all told the same story. "Ugo, does Emmy know?"

"I do not know, Rico. I know of no way to find out short of asking her outright. And I think you do not wish me to do that."

"No, no, of course not." He thought about it a little longer. "Why would Sigrid pay a blackmailer when so many people already know of the affair?"

"She does not know they know. It is supposed to be a secret."

"But if she sends most of her salary to Stockholm, where does she get the money to pay a blackmailer?"

Ugo looked uncomfortable. "Perhaps she steals from Madame Destinn? Some servants do steal, you know. Scandalous!" he finished on a note of righteous indignation.

Caruso hadn't been able to picture Sigrid

with a daughter, but he found he could visualize another image of her quite easily: Sigrid with a knife in her hand, going after Luigi Davila. Suddenly he felt justified in having disliked the woman for so many years.

He sat down at the desk and took out pen and paper. He wrote *Sigrid* at the top of the page in big bold letters. "There, that is one. You say *two* servants may be paying blackmail—who is the other?"

Ugo was uneasy. "You will not like it, Rico."

Caruso sat with pen poised over the paper. "Who is it?"

"You will not like it a *lot*."

"Come, come, Ugo—the name?"

"Mario."

Caruso sighed, put the pen down, swiveled in his chair to face Ugo, and folded his hands placidly in his lap. "Ugo. You cannot put a person on the suspect list just because you do not like that person." *Sigrid is different,* he told himself. "Shame on you, Ugo—trying to get Mario into trouble."

"You always take his part," Ugo said sulkily. "You do not even *listen* to me."

"Eh, well," Caruso sighed again. "I will

listen. What has Mario done to invite the attentions of a blackmailer?"

Ugo threw up his hands. "I do not know! Mario never talks about himself— Mario never talks about *anything*. But Rico, consider. What does he do with his money?"

"His money?"

"Have you ever seen him spend any money? You pay him a good salary, you provide his food and a place to live. You even buy the clothes he wears."

Still harping on the new suit, Caruso thought. "So?"

"So, where does his money go? I spend my money, Martino spends his money, Barthélemy spends his money— but Mario never spends a cent. So what happens to his salary? Perhaps he was turning it over to Luigi Davila?"

"Ugo, you do not know what Mario does with every minute of his time. He could be spending money without your knowing about it."

Ugo shook his head vigorously. "No, Rico, he spends nothing. Ask Martino, if you do not believe me. We have wondered about it many times."

That made a difference; if Martino had

also noticed, then there might be something in what Ugo said. "Perhaps he is saving his money. In a bank."

"He has no bank passbook among his belongings. I looked."

Caruso was shocked. "You searched his belongings?"

"You tell me to investigate," Ugo said sullenly. "I investigate. I am sorry if you do not like what I find."

"Yes, yes, but I do not mean . . ." Well, it was only fair, he supposed; his own servants should be exposed to the same sort of scrutiny as other people's. Caruso didn't for one minute believe innocent young Mario had been paying a blackmailer—but what *did* he do with his money?

"How much do you know about Mario?" Ugo went on. "You know everything there is to know about the rest of us, but you do not really know anything about Mario at all—do you, Rico?"

Caruso had to admit he knew virtually nothing of Mario's background. The young man had been working as a baggage handler in the train station at Milan the first time Caruso ever saw him. The tenor had been so impressed by the boy's nice manners and the efficient way he stacked the suitcases that he'd offered him a job on the spot. And Mario had never given him reason to regret his impulse. He was hard-working, conscientious, self-effacing. Always there when he was wanted and never there when he was not wanted. Mario was, in short, The Perfect Servant. That alone was grounds for suspicion.

But then Caruso thought of something. "Ah— Ugo, Mario cannot have been turning his salary over to Luigi Davila. Davila had not been in the blackmailing business very long when he was killed— so, Mario is innocent!"

Ugo sneered. "You always take Mario's part. You decide he is not guilty because you do not wish him to be guilty. Just like Mr. Puccini."

"Ugo!" Caruso roared so loudly that Martino came running in to see what was the matter. Caruso waved him out with assurances that all was well. Ugo's words had stung; Caruso had to admit there might be some truth in them. Reluctantly he added Mario's name to the list of suspects, more to placate Ugo than out of any conviction of his own. Then he added a big

black question mark after the name.

Partly mollified, Ugo said, "Now what do we do, Rico?"

Caruso smiled wickedly. "I have been thinking about that. A person who has been blackmailed once can be blackmailed twice, yes?"

Ugo shrugged.

"So I was thinking I will write a little note to our suspect if we find one. A note saying that I, an unnamed gentleman, am taking over where Luigi Davila left off. I will say that I, the new blackmailer, have 'inherited' the evidence Davila left behind! What do you think?"

Ugo was frowning. "Did we not decide that the killer removed all the evidence from Davila's office?"

"Ah, but Davila could have made copies! Which he hid someplace else. No blackmail victim can take the chance that there is still evidence somewhere that can hurt her — or him, them."

"And then if our suspect agrees to pay . . ." Ugo's eyes were gleaming. "Yes, I see! It is a good plan, Rico!"

"Yes! Now we must decide how to word the note."

"Oh — I forgot to ask you. Do your own investigations reveal nothing? No suspects?"

Caruso thought for a long time before he answered. Finally he said, "Yes. One suspect."

"Who?"

"Pasquale Amato."

Ugo's face lit up, loving the thought of a new scandal. "Mr. Amato? What — ?"

"Do not ask what he has done because I am not going to tell you. Be content knowing only that it is possible, just possible, that he may have been approached by the blackmailing Mr. Davila."

"It must — "

"Not a word, Ugo! I am not going to tell you." Congratulating himself on his own fair-mindedness, Caruso added his friend's name to the list of suspects. His real motive was considerably less admirable than he liked to think, however. He was certain Amato was innocent of murder; but a note from an unknown blackmailer would give the baritone an uncomfortable moment or two. Caruso chuckled. That should pay him back nicely for the incident of the glued Bible.

He held up his list so Ugo could see: *Sigrid, Mario?, Pasquale.* "I do not send a note to Mario," he announced, "at least, not yet. I talk to him first. If I am not satisfied, then we send him a note."

Ugo nodded unenthusiastically. "What will the note say?"

Caruso thought a moment and then began to write.

Luigi Davila made copies of all his important papers and left them with me for safekeeping. I now offer these papers for sale. If you wish to purchase any part of them, meet me

"Where is a good place?" Caruso asked.

"Some public spot," Ugo said. "Let's see . . . how about Central Park?"

"Too cold."

"Indoors, then. A train station, a museum—"

"A museum! That's it."

at the Metropolitan Museum of Art on Friday, 9 December, at twelve noon. I shall be waiting in the Venetian glass section on the second floor. If you do not wish to purchase these papers, I intend selling them to the newspapers.

"Signature?" Ugo asked.

Caruso placed a black X at the bottom of the page—there, that looked properly mysterious. He copied the letter carefully and took out two envelopes. "What is Sigrid's last name?"

Ugo looked blank. "I don't know."

"Eh, well, there is only one Sigrid backstage at the Met." He wrote *Sigrid* on one envelope and *Pasquale Amato* on the other. "Now Ugo, I want you to deliver these letters tomorrow afternoon during final dress rehearsal. Wait until the rehearsal starts. And be sure to hand them directly to Sigrid and Pasquale—do not leave them lying on a dressing table. Tell each one that a man you do not know stopped you on your way into the opera house and asked you to deliver an envelope. That way neither one will suspect you of having anything to do with it. You understand?"

"Yes, Rico." Ugo took the two letters, his eyes gleaming, excited by the adventure he was involved in. "What if they ask me what the man looks like?"

"Make up something. Describe Lieutenant O'Halloran. Now please tell Martino to prepare the bath. I am ready for a long soak."

"Which scent?"

"It does not matter, anything," Caruso said distractedly. Ugo raised his eyebrows and left. Caruso was excited himself; they were coming down to the wire, as they said at the American racetrack. If everything worked out, Sigrid would show up at the museum on Friday, Caruso would notify Lieutenant O'Halloran, and the murderer would be safely locked up in jail before the curtain opened on the première of *La Fanciulla del West* on Saturday night. Then they could all forget about murder and blackmail and ugly suspicions and concentrate on the important thing— the music.

Caruso finished his bath and called to Mario for a massage. The tenor stretched out on his stomach— no easy task— and Mario's strong young fingers dug into his neck and shoulder muscles. Soon the knots of tension began to loosen. Mario had known nothing about massage when he first joined Caruso. But he'd learned the techniques quickly from Martino, once the older valet's hands had begun to grow arthritic.

Knead, knead, slap, slap. Caruso tried to consider Ugo's suspicions of Mario objectively. Ugo had always been a little resentful of the younger man who had so quickly won his place in the previously closed all-male household. Ugo had made his displeasure clear—but there had never been even a hint of bad feeling between the new valet and Martino. Undoubtedly because of the deferential courtesy Mario always showed the older man.

So, was the problem Mario or was it Ugo? Caruso remembered Pasquale Amato's whimsical description of Ugo as the middle child in the "family"—the one whose role was not clearly defined. Jealous of the new baby. Caruso groaned.

"Do I hurt you, signore?"

"No, no—it feels good, Mario. Continue."

But there remained the problem of the fate of Mario's monthly salary. It was inconceivable to Caruso that the young man could be paying off a blackmailer; there had to be some perfectly simple explanation. What Caruso needed was a subtle and crafty way of finding out from Mario what he did with his money. He thought about the matter a good five minutes and then said,

"Mario, what do you do with your money?"

"Signore?"

"Your monthly salary— what do you spend it on?"

"I send it to my mother and sisters in Milan," the valet said mournfully. "They have no money."

Caruso twisted around and looked up at him. "You send all of it?"

Mario looked positively funereal. "Alas, no. I keep two dollars for myself, for expenses. I have tried to get by without spending anything, but it is very difficult, signore."

Two dollars a month for personal expenses, Caruso thought in amazement. And Mario was feeling guilty about holding back even that small amount. A lot of Europeans in America sent money back home; Caruso cursed himself for not thinking of that. Especially with the example of Sigrid fresh in his mind— sending part of *her* salary to support her illegitimate daughter. Nothing illegitimate about Mario's actions, though. But wait— Ugo would say Mario was lying.

"How do you send the money, Mario? Loose in an envelope?"

"Oh no, signore— that is not safe. Every

220

month I buy a postal money order. I buy one just this morning."

Aha. "Do you know," Caruso said nonchalantly, "I have never bought a postal money order. Is that not strange? I do not even know what one looks like."

"Would you like to see mine?"

"Yes, please, if you do not mind."

"Not at all." Mario wiped his hands on a towel and left the room. He was back immediately with the postal money order.

One glance at the form told Caruso all he needed to know. The order was indeed made out to Mario's mother, and the amount was exactly two dollars less than what the young man earned in a month. And out of those two dollars he'd had to pay the cost of the money order itself.

Caruso handed the form back and sighed. "Mario, why do you not tell me your mother and your sisters are in need? It is good that you take care of your family—but from now on you will keep half of your salary, and you will spend it on yourself. And do not worry, I myself will make up the difference to your mother. She will not have to go without."

Tears of gratitude welled up in the young

valet's eyes. "Oh signore— how can I thank you? You are so good!"

"No, no, I am a pig. I should have found out long ago." Secretly he resolved to add a little something extra to Mario's monthly postal order— once he could figure out a way to manage it all without Ugo's finding out. He broke into Mario's fervent *grazies* to announce, "Now we will say no more about it— it is settled! Let us concentrate on finishing the massage." He stretched out on his stomach again, and felt one hot tear splash on his back.

Scratch one name from the list of suspects.

TEN

"HIP, HIP, HURRAH," David Belasco enunciated with great care.

"Eep, eep, urra," Caruso caroled happily.

Dress rehearsal was due to start in about ten minutes, but Belasco was still trying. He'd given the chorus one final lecture and was now tying up a few loose ends. "Again, please."

Caruso was happy to oblige. He was happy about everything. He had a suspect, he had a plan, the plan was in operation, and soon everyone at the opera house would be thanking him for removing the dark cloud they were all laboring under.

Backstage, the usual last-rehearsal confusion prevailed. Today they would rehearse for the first (and only) time with the full stage sets in place. The costumes were complete, the stage properties were ready. *Everything* was ready. Naturally, everyone was in a state of advanced panic.

"Don't be nervous, Rico," Barthélemy had said nervously.

All four of Caruso's retainers were there; none of them wanted to miss the dress rehearsal, which was often more interesting than the actual performance. Martino kept fussing with Caruso's costume. Mario carried the throat spray, looking even more lugubrious than usual in the midst of such operatic splendor. Ugo kept bouncing up and down on the balls of his feet, excited at being the only one there besides Caruso who knew about that *other* thing going on there today.

"Just be calm," Barthélemy said, fidgeting. "Take deep breaths."

Caruso laughed and clapped his accompanist on the shoulder. "I think *you* are the one who needs to take deep breaths, Barthélemy. Me, I feel wonderful!" Just then an enormous racket broke out on the other side of the stage, making both Barthélemy and Martino jump. "Go see what that noise is, Mario," Caruso ordered. "Give the throat spray to Martino."

Mario hurried away, almost colliding with Pasquale Amato. "Your policeman friend is here, Rico," the baritone said in a rush, "and he is driving our composer to distraction!"

"Lieutenant O'Halloran?"

"The same." Amato had to raise his voice to be heard over the sound of the orchestra tuning up. "I think he is trying to make Puccini crack."

Just then Puccini's voice rose above the backstage clatter: "Do not bother me at a time like this!" The red-faced composer charged out from behind a flat, followed by the derby-clad police detective.

Instinctively Caruso put out a hand to detain O'Halloran, hoping to allow Puccini time to escape. "Lieutenant, there is something I wish to ask you—"

"Not now, Mr. Caruso." O'Halloran shrugged off the restraining hand and followed Puccini down the offstage stairway into the auditorium.

"Why does he pester him now?" Caruso complained. "Surely the lieutenant knows how important today is!"

"That is why," Amato said dryly. "Hoping to catch him off-guard, no doubt."

Mario returned from his errand. "The horses have arrived," he announced tragically.

They all trooped across the stage to take a look at the horses, Caruso's spurs clanking noisily. Emmy Destinn and a large black mare were eyeing each other distrustfully. When Emmy practiced mounting, Caruso saw she was wearing cotton stockings — eh, Belasco had won that one, then. The mare stretched back and tried to bite the soprano's ankle.

"I want a different horse!" Emmy announced in no uncertain terms, sliding off her mount.

For the first time it occurred to Caruso that the exposure of Sigrid as the murderer would be a great shock to Emmy. She was fond of her maid, in a strange sort of way. Caruso's good mood was momentarily dampened; he did not wish to cause Emmy pain. But he could see no way around it; they would all just have to be especially kind to Emmy when the news broke. Suddenly he realized the normally highly visible maid was nowhere in sight. "Have you seen Sigrid?" he whispered to Ugo.

"Not yet," Ugo whispered back. "But do

not worry, Rico, I will find her."

"What are these horses doing here?" a horrified voice cried. Gatti-Casazza elbowed his way through the crowd. "They are not supposed to be here now! Which of you is in charge?"

One of the animal handlers stepped forward. "This here's the Metropolitan Opera, ain't it? I got an order to deliver eight horses—"

"Yes, yes, but not *now*—they are not needed until the third act! Oh dear!" Gatti-Casazza stared at a steaming pile on the floor. "We can't have these animals back-stage during the entire performance! Take them outside—right now, please."

"Cold out there," the handler grumbled. "Not good for the horses, either."

"But surely you have vans? What did you bring them in?"

"They're open vans, not much protection."

"Then please see to it that Saturday night you have the proper kind of van, the kind that does offer protection. As for now, you'll simply have to improvise something. We can't have all these animals here while we're trying to put on an opera!"

"Well, I s'pose we could double-blanket 'em."

"You do that. And somebody clean up that mess!" The handler and his assistants started moving the horses out. "Oh dear, we should have started by now!" Gatti-Casazza exclaimed, combing his beard nervously with his fingers. "Will you take your places, please? Everyone off the stage who does not belong on the stage!"

Caruso turned to his accompanist. "Barthélemy, take Mario out front and watch from there. And Mario, try to smile once in a while. Martino— why not join them? I do not think— "

"I stay here," Martino said firmly. "You may need me."

Caruso knew better than to argue. He drew Ugo aside and said, low, "I change my mind about one thing. Do not deliver Pasquale's letter until the rehearsal is finished— I do not wish to throw his performance off. But Sigrid's letter can be delivered any time you find her alone. If she is here."

Ugo answered by digging an elbow into Caruso's ribs and gesturing theatrically with his head. The tenor followed his look— and there was Sigrid, arguing with Emmy, as always. That was all right, then.

"I am starting this rehearsal in exactly thirty seconds," a voice from the orchestra pit announced. "The rest of you may join me or not, as you please." Toscanini smiled in satisfaction at the mad rush his words caused. The stage lights went down; the only thing visible was the glowing end of a burning cigar. The first hair-raising chords sounded from the orchestra. The stage lights slowly went up to reveal Amato and one of the miners in the saloon. Dress rehearsal was under way.

Caruso put Sigrid and the letters at the back of his mind and anxiously watched the stage action. The fight went smoothly; no one got hurt. The Bible opened the way it was supposed to. Caruso made his entrance; and when Amato knocked his drink off the bar, no one got splashed. The singing was true, the orchestra was authoritative, the music was beautiful.

The first act of *La Fanciulla del West* was the longest, running about an hour. When Caruso left the stage, he had sweat off all his make-up and hurried upstairs to apply more. Martino handed him a towel and then knelt down to oil Caruso's spurs. "Mr. Belasco's orders," he said apologetically.

"Where is Ugo?" Caruso asked.

"Here." Ugo stood in the doorway, shaking his head *no*. He hadn't been able to deliver the letter yet. Ugo stepped back from the door and Puccini rushed in, followed by Lieutenant O'Halloran.

"Caruso," the composer cried, "if you keep singing like that I will have to rename the opera *The Lad of the Golden West!* Divine!"

"Emmy won't like that," the tenor laughed. "You are satisfied, then?"

"I am *enchanted!* I have never seen a dress rehearsal go so smoothly—especially the final rehearsal for a *new* opera. Ah, if only all rehearsals were like this one! I must speak to Amato and Madame Destinn." He hurried out, not even looking at Lieutenant O'Halloran as he passed; Puccini had decided to deal with the policeman by ignoring him.

"Why don't you leave him alone?" Caruso hissed. O'Halloran only smiled and followed Puccini out. Caruso finished putting on his make-up and hurried downstairs.

The stage set of the girl's cabin was in place for Act II. Except for the brief appearance of a few of the minor characters, this middle section of *Fanciulla* was carried entirely by the three principals. And of those three, only Emmy Destinn was on-stage during the entire act, a total of forty-five minutes. A good time for Ugo to deliver the letter to Sigrid.

Only one small mishap marred the act: The cabin door stuck. Toscanini halted the rehearsal while the stagehands got the door open, and then the act proceeded smoothly to its conclusion. Caruso rushed off, needing to apply make-up for the third time that day.

At the bottom of the stairs to the dressing rooms stood Ugo, smiling broadly and nodding. Sigrid had the letter.

Up the stairs, into the dressing room. Gatti-Casazza visited him briefly, full of effusive compliments. Even David Belasco stopped by with a kind word, no longer miffed by Caruso's invasion of his private rooms. Like most people, Belasco quickly forgot past offenses when he heard Caruso sing.

The last act was the shortest of the three, less than half an hour. Caruso considered the entire opera to be a much more sensible length than those ten-hour marathons Richard Wagner used to churn out, not that any good Italian ever listened to them anyway. Act III of *Fanciulla* opened on a somber picture of dawn breaking over a mountainous forest; and not too long after that, the lynch-minded mob picked out a tree and threw a rope over one limb.

Something was wrong. It wasn't the chorus; they were behaving themselves nicely. The horses weren't doing anything they weren't supposed to be doing. No, the problem was Pasquale Amato. He was angry; he was acting angry and he was *singing* angry. What was the matter? Caruso finished *Ch'ella mi creda*, and Amato marched over to deliver the make-believe slap they'd rehearsed so carefully. Only Amato didn't make believe. He belted Caruso a good one.

The tenor stood there in a state of absolute shock. His non-violent friend had struck him!

Just in time, Emmy came riding to the rescue, fighting her cranky black mare all the way. The lynch mob went back to being just a bunch of miners again and set Caruso free; and a little fancy footwork on the part of the tenor enabled him to keep Emmy between himself and Amato. Then hero and heroine went off together arm-in-arm, singing *"Addio, mia California!"* all the way.

It was over.

laughing, pleased with her performance. Ugo was there, eyes shining in excitement. David Belasco was offering congratulalions all around.

But their moment of triumph was shattered by a woman's voice, screaming abuse — at Caruso! Sigrid came charging toward him, waving a piece of paper over her head. Quickly he hid behind Emmy. Sigrid was shaking his note at him — how had she found out he'd written it? Ugo was looking as startled as Caruso felt. The tenor couldn't understand what Sigrid was saying, but he was pretty sure he was hearing some choice Swedish swearing.

Then a new stream of abuse started from behind him — and this time it was in Italian and Caruso *could* understand it. He turned to see Pasquale Amato advancing toward him, and *he* was waving a piece of paper over *his* head! *Per dio!* What had gone wrong?

"I told you to hold Pasquale's until *after* the rehearsal!" Caruso yelled at Ugo.

"I was afraid I would miss him!" Ugo yelled back.

Caruso was trying to use Emmy to fend off both Sigrid and Amato, but the soprano had had enough and broke away. "What *is* all this?" she demanded. Suddenly Barthélemy and Martino and Mario were there, and Toscanini and Gatti-Casazza, and Puccini and Lieutenant O'Halloran. Caruso felt himself being backed out onto the stage.

"This time you go too far, Rico!" Amato shouted angrily. "What a vulgar, stupid joke!" He read from the note: " 'Luigi Davila made copies of all his important papers and left them with me for safe-keeping . . .' "

"What's this? What's this?" Lieutenant O'Halloran pushed his way to the front of the crowd.

"That's the same thing mine says!" Sigrid exclaimed. She and Amato compared letters.

They were all out on the stage, including the chorus and the rest of the cast, who had come back to see what was going on. Caruso couldn't stand it any longer. "How did you know?" he wailed. "How did both of you know I wrote those letters?"

"Don't be foolish," Amato growled. "I'd know that scrawl of yours anywhere—it's unmistakable. Nobody else writes quite like that. I could tell just from reading my name on the envelope that the note was from you."

"Chicken scratches," Sigrid snorted.

Caruso shot a quick glance at Ugo's startled face looking over David Belasco's shoulder. They'd neither of them thought of that! Caruso's talent for subterfuge did not extend to disguising his handwriting.

"Let me see those letters," Lieutenant O'Halloran commanded. Sigrid and Amato handed them over. Toscanini edged up to the policeman and read them with him. He threw a reproving look at Caruso and made a clucking sound with his tongue.

"Will someone please explain to me what is happening here?" Gatti-Casazza cried plaintively.

O'Halloran scratched his neck uneasily. "Well, on the face of it, it would appear that your star tenor is trying to blackmail your star baritone and this lady here." The police detective was clearly puzzled. "Now why would you do a thing like that, Mr. Caruso?"

"There is some mistake!" Gatti-Casazza gasped. "Someone else wrote those letters!"

Caruso smiled sadly. "No, Mr. Gatti, there is no mistake. I wrote the letters — both of them."

Amato was shaking his finger under Caruso's nose. "What a *tasteless* thing to do, Rico! Using a dead man to pay me back for one little trick I play on you! You should be whipped!"

"Do not speak to Rico like that!" the loyal Martino called out. Mario looked as if he wanted to cry.

"What are you talking about, a trick?" Sigrid asked Amato. "I play no tricks on anyone!"

"I am sorry, Pasquale," Caruso said, honestly contrite. "It was wrong of me to do what I did. I beg your forgiveness."

He looked so miserable that Amato didn't have the heart to stay mad at him. "Eh, well, no harm done, I suppose. But never do a thing like that again!"

"Never," Caruso promised solemnly.

"You see what comes of playing tricks?" Toscanini announced to the world at large. "Nothing but trouble!"

"Tricks, tricks, tricks!" Sigrid cried in exasperation. "What have tricks to do with me?"

"Mr. Caruso," Lieutenant O'Halloran said, "don't you think it's time you explained?"

Almost eighty faces were staring at him, waiting for a little speech that would magically make everything clear. Caruso swallowed hard and plunged in. "I investigate the murder of Luigi Davila. The police seem content to think our friend Puccini is the guilty party—but I am not content, no! I know Puccini has killed no one. I know he did not put that knife in Davila's side. So I decide I will find out who did!"

"Oh, Caruso!" Puccini said so softly that only Barthélemy heard him.

"Just exactly how did you go about your investigating?" O'Halloran asked, half-irritated, half-amused.

"I listen, I ask questions, I read things." Caruso shrugged. "I . . . *investigate.*"

"That is why you were going through the papers in my desk," Belasco said suddenly.

"And that is why you were hiding in my wardrobe cabinet!" Emmy exclaimed.

237

"Is that why you followed me every-where?" Gatti-Casazza wanted to know. "To find out if I was a murderer?"

Caruso started to sweat. "Well, uh, a detective must be impartial . . ."

"Rico!" Emmy cried. "Do you really think I could be a murderer?"

"No, Emmy, no!" he hastened to assure her. "I investigate you to prove you are *not* a murderer! I eliminate suspects, one by one!" Emmy didn't really believe that, but she decided to let him get away with it. For the time being.

"So you eliminated everybody until you got down to Mr. Amato and the lady — Sigrid, is it?" O'Halloran said. "Then you wrote letters to these two. Mr. Caruso, exactly what did you expect these letters to accomplish?"

How to word it without implicating Puccini before all these nosy people? "You know Luigi Davila was a blackmailer," Caruso said carefully. "He could have had many victims the police do not know about— and it is likely that one of them killed him, yes? I think if I pretend to take over where Davila left off, the killer will reveal herself . . . or himself."

"I see." O'Halloran studied Caruso. "Now suppose you tell me why you think these two people here were Luigi Davila's blackmail victims?"

Amato was staring at the tenor in horror. "You think that Davila was blackmailing *me?* You think *I* am the one who killed him?"

"No, no, Pasquale! I never think that! Not even for one little moment!" He had determined never to give his friend away; this was the test. "It is only that I see a chance to get even with you — for the Bible trick. That is all, I assure you!"

Belasco gaped at Amato. "The Bible trick? *You* glued the pages of the Bible together?"

"What are you talking about?" O'Halloran wanted to know.

Toscanini looked hurt. "Not you too, Amato! Always tricks!"

Amato shrugged, started to explain, but then decided not to bother.

Gatti-Casazza told Lieutenant O'Halloran about the Bible. "So this letter you wrote to Mr. Amato," the police detective said to Caruso, "was by way of being retaliation for a practical joke he played on you? Is that it?"

"Yes," Caruso said miserably, "and I am filled with shame at what I do! I am through playing tricks — forever!"

Toscanini brightened. "Swear!"

Right then and there Caruso took a solemn oath to abstain from playing practical jokes for the rest of his life, and a few people even believed him. "So you see, Lieutenant O'Halloran, it is all a stupid mistake. I have no *reason* to suspect Pasquale — he has done nothing he could be blackmailed for!" He would take his friend's guilty secret with him to the grave.

"Which leaves Sigrid," O'Halloran said pointedly.

The already pale Swedish woman turned even whiter, her mouth working noiselessly. She swallowed and said, "I? You think I killed a man?"

"I do not know," Caruso said in anguish. Now that it had come to the point of actually accusing the woman outright, he was having all sorts of doubts.

"But you thought she might be vulnerable to blackmail," O'Halloran cut in sharply. "Why, Mr. Caruso? What did you find out that made you write her that letter?"

Caruso wished he were any place in the

world other than where he was at the moment. He didn't like Sigrid any more now than he'd ever liked her, but when it came down to calling her a murderer – Caruso decided right then he just wasn't hard-hearted enough to make a good detective.

But Lieutenant O'Halloran was insisting upon an answer.

Caruso directed his reply to Sigrid. "I find out about your illegitimate child," he said in a tone of apology. "The little girl in Sweden you are supporting."

"Oh no!" Emmy Destinn shrieked before Sigrid could say a word. "Not that ugly story *again!* Rico, you should know better than to listen to backstage gossip! Shame on you!"

Caruso looked at her in bewilderment. "You know about it?"

"I know about the child," Emmy snapped, "and I also know she is neither illegitimate nor Sigrid's. Sigrid is supporting her widowed sister's child – her *niece,* you fool, not her daughter!"

Caruso groaned as a murmur ran through the crowd. Sigrid pressed her lips together and lifted her chin defiantly.

241

"Rico, why didn't you ask me?" Emmy went on. "I could have told you. Sigrid was with me in London when the girl was born— *in Stockholm.* This story about the 'illegitimate' daughter has appeared before — spread by idle, no-good servants who have nothing better to do than make up malicious lies about a good woman! And you listened! Rico, I could kill you!"

Caruso wanted nothing more than for the stage floor to open up and swallow him whole. What an injustice he had done the woman! How quick he had been to suspect her— just because they had never gotten along well together! He rushed over to Sigrid and started pouring out his apologies.

Sigrid listened to his final appeal for forgiveness and then rewarded him with an icy smile. "I will think about it." Caruso envisioned long years of doing penance to Emmy Destinn's maid.

"That's what comes of meddling," Amato whispered. The crowd divided as Emmy and Sigrid made a regal exit from the stage.

Puccini stepped up and placed a hand on Caruso's shoulders. "You are in this predicament because of me," he said. "I want you to know that whatever happens,

I will always be grateful to you, Caruso."

O'Halloran took off his derby, wiped his forehead with the back of his hand, replaced the derby. "From now on I think you'd better stick to singing, Mr. Caruso. Leave the detective work to the police. Don't meddle."

Caruso nodded emphatic agreement. "My career as a detective is finished." The crowd of people on the stage was beginning to thin out; the show was over. Toscanini left, followed by a shaky Gatti-Casazza leaning on David Belasco's arm.

Martino came up to Caruso. "Are you all right, Rico?" Ugo and Barthélemy and Mario crowded around them; everybody wanted to go home.

"As a point of curiosity, Rico," Amato said, "what would you have done if I had brought the money?"

"Eh? What money?"

"The money you ask for in the letter."

"I do not ask for money in the letter."

"Of course you do. Look here." Amato took one of the letters from Lieutenant O'Halloran. "See—right there."

Caruso looked at the letter. The part arranging for a meeting in the art museum had been crossed out. At the bottom of the page one sentence had been printed in block letters:

> *Leave $10,000 wrapped in newspaper in the properties room of the opera house Saturday night and you will never hear from me again.*

"But I do not write this!" Caruso cried. "What I write is up here—with the line drawn through it! I ask for a meeting, that is all! I know nothing about this demand for ten thousand dollars!"

"I was wondering why part of the letter was written and part printed," Amato scowled.

"Both letters are like that," Lieutenant O'Halloran pointed out. "Except that this other one asks for only a thousand—that must be Sigrid's. Mr. Caruso, are you saying somebody else added this sentence about the money?"

"Yes! I do not even know about it until right now!"

"But who?"

"Who indeed? I write the letters last night and then . . ." And then? Caruso's eyes automatically turned to Ugo—the only other person who knew about the letters.

Ugo bolted.

"Stop him!" O'Halloran shouted. "Stop that man!"

A few lingering chorus members turned to see what this new fuss was about and unwittingly blocked the exit. Ugo skittered to a stop and turned to dash back across the stage. He ducked away from Amato, pushed Puccini aside, and tried to jump into the orchestra pit—but Lieutenant O'Halloran got a hand on him. Ugo pulled away and next tried to dart past Caruso. The tenor deliberately stepped into his path, and the resulting collision took both men to the floor.

Caruso prevented Ugo's escape by the simple expedient of sitting on him.

"Oof! *Dio*, you are crushing me! Get up, Rico!"

"Ugo," Caruso said sadly, "you have been very naughty. Trying to extort money from my friend! For shame."

"I think maybe he's been more than naughty," Lieutenant O'Halloran said, hunkering down by the fallen valet. "All right, you—what's your name? Ugo? What do you know about all this?"

"Rico, I am dying! Let me up!"

"I let you up when you tell the truth. Answer Lieutenant O'Halloran."

"Did you add that sentence to the letters, Ugo?" O'Halloran asked. "The one asking for money?"

"Yes! Yes! Now let me up!"

"Do you go in for blackmail a lot, Ugo?"

"This is the first time! My bones are breaking!"

"But you don't mind helping yourself to other people's money? Maybe you even steal a little?"

Ugo sobbed. Caruso gave a little bounce. "Yes, yes— I steal!"

"From Mr. Caruso here?"

"For six years I steal from him! And he never suspects a thing!"

Caruso's mouth dropped open. "You steal from me?"

"Ugo," O'Halloran said in an ominously quiet voice, "did you kill Luigi Davila?"

Ugo didn't answer. O'Halloran and Caruso exchanged a look, and the police detective nodded. Caruso shifted his weight.

Ugo cried out. "Yes, yes, I kill him! Why do you torture me! I kill him! I say so!"

"*Cielo!*" Amato whispered.

Caruso was so stunned that O'Halloran had to tell him twice to let Ugo go. The tenor moved his buttocks to the stage floor; Ugo rolled over on his back, gasping for air. Puccini walked over to stand by Ugo's head, looking down at him but saying nothing.

Martino didn't understand what had just happened. "What is it? What does he say?" Barthélemy patted him on the shoulder and spoke low into his ear. When Martino understood, he began to cry.

Caruso felt like crying himself. "Ugo, how could you? How could you kill a man?"

Ugo struggled up to a sitting position. "I do not intend to kill him—it was an accident!"

O'Halloran used one thumb to push his derby to the back of his head. "An accident. The knife just accidentally went off in your hand?"

"He attacked *me*," Ugo said sullenly. "I must defend myself, yes?"

"So now it's self-defense. Let's back up a little. Davila was trying to blackmail *you*—is that the way it was?"

"Something like that," Ugo mumbled. "He wanted half of everything I got."

"But I do not understand," Caruso

protested. "How were you able to steal from me? I write down everything I spend!"

"And you think that is all there is to it!" Ugo sneered. "You write down a number on a piece of paper, and everything is magically taken care of! Rico, what do you do with those pieces of paper after you write your little figures on them?"

"I give them to you," Caruso said heavily.

"You give them to me. *I* have to pay the bills, *I* am the one who keeps track of where the money goes! You have never appreciated how hard I work for you, Rico!"

"How hard you work at cheating him, you mean," Amato said dryly.

"How did Davila find out?" O'Halloran asked.

"A cousin of his sells linens," Ugo said. "The cousin tells him about the little arrangement he has with me. I order from him and he overcharges—then he and I share the overcharge, yes? The cousin, he is pleased with the way we do business and he wants to brag a little to his relative—you see?"

"Uh-huh. And maybe you had this same arrangement with a few other merchants? How many, Ugo?" Ugo did not answer, pouting. *"How many?"* O'Halloran roared.

"Seventeen, maybe twenty. I do not remember exactly."

Caruso was outraged. So many people conspiring to cheat him out of his money! He was tempted to bang Ugo in the shin with one of his spurs.

"So then what?" O'Halloran went on. "Davila asked around, found out which merchants you deal with?"

"He must have," Ugo said unhappily. "He knew the names of— oh, quite a few. But to demand half! It is too much. I go see him, I try to talk him into taking less. He is sitting there on his bed peeling a small apple with a large knife. He refuses to take less than half. He becomes angry, I become angry— we fight. He puts his hands around my neck"— Ugo raised both hands to his throat to demonstrate— "and I am afraid! I grab the knife and . . . I do not mean to kill him! I swear it!"

A long silence followed, broken only by an occasional sob from Ugo. Then Lieutenant O'Halloran said, "Did you take any letters or other papers out of Davila's office?"

"I take nothing. I think only of getting

away— I do not think of *papers.*"

"No other blackmail victims, then," O'Halloran muttered. "That's one good thing."

"So I was wrong about that, too!" Caruso moaned. "What a hypocrite you are, Ugo! All that time, you are just pretending to help me look for the killer! First you pretend you have trouble remembering who Davila is, and then you pretend to search out his address— so *I* will be the one to find him dead! Then you 'investigate'— while you know all along *you* are the one I am looking for!"

"You said there might be other people Davila was blackmailing," the valet answered sullenly.

"And you look for one to put the blame on. First you blame Puccini, and then Sigrid. Ugo, believe me, I can understand how a man might kill in the heat of a fight— if he is frightened enough. But to allow another person to be punished for it— oh, Ugo! Of all the things you do— stealing from me, killing Luigi Davila, trying to blackmail Pasquale— I think the worst thing is incriminating an innocent person. For that, I never forgive you!"

"Ugo?" said a feminine voice from the side of the stage. "Ugo killed that man?" Caruso turned his head to see Emmy Destinn, now changed into street clothes. She looked straight at the tenor, still sitting on the floor. "*Your* servant is the killer—instead of *my* servant?"

"That's right, ma'am," Lieutenant O'Halloran answered her. "Mr. Caruso's valet here is the one we've been looking for."

Caruso groaned. "I harbor a criminal in my own household!" With a great straining of muscles he got up from the floor. "Emmy, I am so sorry I accuse Sigrid! I am desolate! I—"

"Don't." She held up a hand to stop him and then walked over to where he was standing. "Do not apologize—I am no longer angry, Rico. In fact, I have come to thank you."

"Thank me?"

"Yes. If you had not accused Sigrid, then I would never have been able to explain the truth about the child before the entire company. So you see, you have done Sigrid a favor!"

"Get up," O'Halloran said to Ugo.

251

"And now that everybody knows the truth about Sigrid's niece," Emmy continued, "there will be no more of that ugly gossip! I am grateful to you, Rico— thank you!" Emmy gave the astonished tenor a warm hug. She shot one appalled look at Ugo and started to leave. "Take care of your voice, Rico!" she trilled, and was gone.

"Well!" Amato said with a big smile. "That worked out nicely, didn't it?"

Puccini was talking to O'Halloran. "What is my status now, Lieutenant?"

"I'd say you were completely off the hook, Mr. Puccini. I have to talk to the district attorney, but I doubt he'll even need you to testify at the inquest now. And Mr. Caruso, I take back what I said. If you hadn't meddled in the case, all this would never have come to light. You helped me catch a killer, and you helped yourself, too— you're lucky to get this scum out of your house." He took out a pair of handcuffs. "Come here, you," he said to Ugo.

Caruso did a little dance. "Eh, Pasquale! What do you say to my 'meddling' now?"

"I will say this," Amato laughed, shaking his head, "you are one of a kind, Rico!"

Caruso lowered his voice so the others

wouldn't hear. "And I do it all without letting anyone else find out about your secret!"

"My secret? What secret is that?"

Caruso looked around to make sure no one was listening. "I know about *Francesca!*"

Amato raised his eyebrows and, surprisingly, smiled. "Oh? Is she writing to you too now?"

The tenor looked at him blankly. "Why would your wife write to me?"

"Francesca is not my wife! You know my wife's name is Rosa."

"But Francesca signs her letter 'Your loving and faithful wife'!"

"Rico, have you been reading my mail?" Amato asked in helpless exasperation.

"No, no—just the one letter." Caruso decided to take the offensive. "You should not leave letters like that lying around in a closed drawer where anyone can find them! Why does she call herself your wife? Who is this Francesca?"

Amato smiled wryly. "I do not know—I have never met her! I do not even know her last name. Our Francesca likes to fantasize—pretending we are married and all the rest of it. She is just a woman who enjoys writing *that* kind of letter." He grinned. "As I enjoy reading it."

"A *fan?!*" Caruso said incredulously.

"A fan," his friend nodded. "She writes to me in every city where I sing—for two years now she has been writing. Except once, in Paris, there was no letter." Amato sighed. "I rather missed hearing from her."

"A fan," Caruso repeated, dumbfounded. "*I* never get letters like that! *My* fans write asking for money." He shook himself, thoroughly ashamed that he had ever believed his friend to be a bigamist. "Does your wife know you get these letters?"

"*Dio,* no!" Amato said, shocked. "She would kill me!"

Lieutenant O'Halloran was ready to take his prisoner in. "Well, that should wrap it up. And Mr. Caruso, if you ever decide to play detective again—come to me when you find something, will you, instead of going off on your own? Good luck to all of you Saturday night. Come on, you." He hauled Ugo unceremoniously away.

"Signore!" Mario stood at a respectful distance, looking more funereal than ever. "You do not mean what you say, do you? About never forgiving Ugo?"

Caruso was surprised to see real tears in the valet's sad young eyes. "Do you think I should forgive him, Mario?"

"Ugo is not a happy man, signore— and unhappy people do not make wise decisions. In all the time I know him, I never once see him happy." Mario scrunched up his face, holding back the tears. "I know *I* make him unhappy."

Caruso shook his head. "Mario, Ugo would manage to be discontent whether you are there or not. You are not to blame for his unhappiness . . . nor am I. Ugo himself is the cause of his problems." Caruso glanced over to where Barthélemy was trying to console Martino, who still looked upset. "I worry about Martino— see if you can cheer him up, Mario." Sending mournful Mario to cheer anyone up struck him as slightly ludicrous, but he wanted to give the young man something to do.

Amato smiled as he watched the three remaining members of Caruso's household trying to make one another feel better. "You are a good papa, Rico."

A throat-clearing sound made them both turn. Puccini was watching Caruso, looking both awed and humble— something neither singer had ever seen before. "Caruso," the composer said simply, "I owe you my life!"

"Oh, you exaggerate, my friend," Caruso said in a totally unsuccessful attempt at modesty.

"I owe you my freedom, and that is the same as my life," Puccini answered. "I do not know anyone else who would do for me what you have done. What risks you must have taken!"

"Only a few," Caruso said, pleased, resisting the urge to bow.

"To take it upon yourself to go out and look for a *murderer!*" Puccini shook his head in amazement. "Incredible!"

"*I* advised him to mind his own business," Amato sighed.

"Then I thank God he did not listen to your advice! I would be in jail within a week if he . . . Caruso, how can I thank you? I am indebted to you for the rest of my life—I owe you everything!"

"No, no, you must not feel that way!" Caruso cried. "You owe me nothing! What I do, I do out of friendship. There is no question of 'owing' me anything!"

Puccini smiled slowly. "Yes, you do see it that way, do you not? I think you must be the most generous-spirited man in the world." The composer's smile broadened; he held out his arms. "Enrico!"

Caruso held out his arms in return. "Giacomo!"

The two men embraced— and passionately pledged their undying friendship, in the grandest of grand opera traditions.

On Saturday evening, December 10, 1910, *La Fanciulla del West* premièred at the Metropolitan Opera House in New York City. Nothing disastrous happened; the performance went as smooth as clockwork. The first-night audience was overwhelmed. Cast, conductor, and composer took a total of fifty-two curtain calls.

Fifty-two.

The publishers hope that this Large Print Book has brought you pleasurable reading. Each title is designed to make the text as easy to see as possible. G. K. Hall Large Print Books are available from your library and your local bookstore. Or you can receive information on upcoming and current Large Print Books by mail and order directly from the publisher. Just send your name and address to:

G. K. Hall & Co.
70 Lincoln Street
Boston, Mass. 02111

or call, toll-free:

1-800-343-2806

A note on the text
Large print edition designed by
Bernadette Montalvo
Composed in 16 pt Plantin
on an EditWriter 7700
by Marilyn Ann Richards of G. K. Hall Corp.